Your Wife is Good...Now get back in Your Bed

Alisha finally gets it but does she do the right thing

The Clean-Up Woman Chronicles

4

Copyright 2013 Holloman Publishing
ISBN-10: 0989727432
ISBN-13: 978-0-9897274-3-3

Special thanks

To all of my supporters

This book is dedicated to relationship in every condition, good or bad. I hope you see your way through.

Table of contents

Introduction

The final leg of Alisha's journey on her life choices or is it?

Alisha has endured several life changing obstacles because of her choices and lack of self-control but has she learned a lesson yet or is she willing to let a broken heart and a sexual lust drive her in the wrong direction again? Alisha is a bright woman so life experiences and age should guide her in a different direction.

This was a fictional story with real life issues that people deal with every day and no one is above dealing with life choices whether its positive or negative but we must look at each moment as half full or enjoy today because tomorrow is not certain but if it is we will be better than today. We must live each day to the fullest as we learn from our mistakes and grow instead of hide from them.

This book was fictional but encompassed real life stories. Whether you're the cheater, been cheated on or a willing accomplice to a cheater this book should give you a revelation. What are you allowing to be done and what are you doing with your life? It's time out for the blame game and finger pointing on your life choices. If you knew your mate was a cheater before you married them don't complain because they showed you who they were and you chose not to believe them; which makes you an accomplice. If you wore a mask until the day you were married you're a manipulator or deceiver, so you caused your mate to seek what they thought they were getting from you in someone else. If you knew they were married before you went the extra mile you can only blame yourself and mates can only blame their mates because they are the ones that owe you that honesty and trust.

Regrets of A Dream

As I walked into the hospital room I smiled at Mr. Avery manning his post, watching Alonzo waiting for him to awake. "Hi dad, how are you?" He looked tired. "Was there any movement today?"

Mr. Avery sighed, "No, but he grunted a little when the nurse was changing the bedding."

I tried to give him a supportive smile before I gave words of encouragement. "Well that sounds promising."

"Alisha I keep telling you these things are involuntary…"

"Dad if you feel that way, why are you posted by his bedside every day?"

"Just in case he wakes up I want someone to be here."

"Well you should celebrate the little things and have faith that those things will lead to Alonzo waking up."

"Faith is your department I believe in what I can see." He laughed. I kissed him on the cheek before he departed. I walked over to my husband's bedside and sighed as I sat down.

During my visits I would talk to Alonzo about the children and Tommy practicing for their next round of golf. After three hours of talking about everything his hand moved. "Oh my God baby, don't worry I'll get a nurse." Jumping up I pressed the call button. I quickly grabbed his hand, "Alonzo, are you waking up?" I called out to him as a nurse walked in and frowned. "Mrs. Avery like I told your father his movements are involuntary and not a sign of real movement see look at the..." She paused and ran towards the door," I need assistance in room 4-8-0!" Before the other nurses could respond Alonzo sat up and the machines started going off. "Baby you're awake." I said as I ran toward his bedside and to embrace him. "Mrs. Avery we need for you to step out of the room for just a moment," a nurse said. I blew a kiss at Alonzo and told him I love him. I pulled out my phone to call Mr. Avery as I walked out the room. "Dad he's awake," I screamed. "What?"
"Alonzo just woke up so get back..." before I

could finish I heard a familiar sound and all I could do was think about Papa and Grams as I felt the contents of my stomach trying to exit my mouth. I turned and look through the window and screamed, "Noooo!" A nurse ran into his room with a cart. I could hear a familiar voice and realized it was Mr. Avery on the phone. I slowly gathered my thoughts, "Hey Dad."

"What's going on Alisha?"

"I don't know."

"Is my son still alive?"

"I don't know." I said again as if I were dreaming and everything was going in slow motion. Suddenly a man was in front of me but he had to shake me before I responded. "Yes, I'm Mrs. Avery his wife."

"Mr. Avery had a slight heart attack but he is fine. We want to monitor him closer so we are going to take him to ICU until further notice."

"When are you going to move him and what are the visiting hours?" I said as if I were in a fog.

"Mrs. Avery the Charge Nurse will assist you with any questions you may have." A tall slim dark complexion older lady with her hair in a bun escorted me into a room as I glanced back to see Alonzo through the glass window. We talked for a few moments and she handed me some papers. After

speaking with her I called Mr. Avery back.
"Dad we can't see him until nine o'clock in
the morning."
"What, they can't stop me from seeing my
son." He yelled.
"Dad, Alonzo sustained some severe
injuries so when he awake his body went
into shock causing him to have a mild heart
attack. They want to observe him closer so
they can monitor him without interruption."
"Okay Alisha I'll just go up there in the
morning." We hung up not realizing what
the day held.

When I arrived home to check on the
kids I saw that Mr. Avery's car was not
there. I sat in my car for a few moments
because my stomach was in knots. I opened
the car door but my phone rang, "Hello." I
closed the door and drove off. When I
walked into the room my heart sank
because I lost my husband before we could
share a life together. Alonzo was gone and I
felt as if time had stopped, twirled me
around, and deposited me in misery. I loved
Alonzo and I had finally given up Julian to
be with him. Alonzo died of a blood clot that
lodged in his lungs

Two months later Ginger was sentenced
to a life term plus 20 years to be served
consecutively because she endangered

children. Mr. Avery wanted her to die in the gas chamber. After Alonzo's funeral he stayed at Alonzo's house and didn't want anyone to come over. Ms. Daniels was stressed but wanted to continue to take care of the children. She needed to take her mind off the whole situation and her babies kept her busy. It was hard to bury another husband. Millie was crushed so she wouldn't eat for days after his death. Alonzo's death cast a shadow over our home for a while.

Almost a year after Alonzo's death things started to settle out and our home was almost normal again. Millie was running around the house playing with her brothers. After AJ turned a year old, we had a small, family only, birthday party for him. Tommy and his family, Ms. Daniels, her daughter Naomi, and her kids were the only people invited. Olivia decided to come at the last minute because she realized we were the only family she had. After the party I was exhausted and for some reason all I could think about was Julian; my obsession for him had returned six months ago, so I tried not to accept the fact that I needed help. After I spoke with the agents all I could do was wonder if I had done something different would Julian still be here. I would go to sleep dreaming of him and wake up to an empty bed, so I would go check on the kids before I tried to go back to sleep. I felt guilty because Alonzo was right about my obsession with Julian. I knew Ms. Daniels had begun to pray over me and anoint my room every night, but I pretended as if I didn't know because it meant so much to her.

One night I awoke after hearing a loud thud I arose from my pile of pillows that I slept on pretending they were Julian and reached for my gun. I looked around and didn't see anything so I went back to sleep. I was thinking when will I stop having this dream when I turned to see Ms. Daniels on the floor. "Ms. Daniels, are you okay?" I asked rushing to her side. She began to moan as she rose from the floor. "Alisha I saw Julian in the bed with you."
"Ms. Daniels, I was in the bed alone."
"No Alisha, his eyes were open and he spoke."
"Ms. Daniels I was sleeping on a pile of pillows and I have his picture on them so I can pretend its Julian."
Ms. Daniels slowly rose from the floor with my assistance. She sat on the bed and sighed, "Alisha I'm not losing my mind."
"Ms. Daniels I'm not saying that but I was

in the bed alone." I thought am I still dreaming again. I pinched myself as usual.

"Alisha what are you doing?"

"Trying to see if I'm dreaming."

"Well pinch me too because I'm seeing things." We laughed as she stood up to leave.

"Ms. Daniels why were you in here anyway?" I knew why but for some reason I needed her to say it.

"Child since Julian died I've been coming in here covering you in prayer. I stopped after you and Alonzo started dating but after his death I started doing it again."

"Why?"

"Ma Carrie told me about your past and how the enemy is always attacking you, so it went from once a month to once a week. After the events over the past year with Alonzo it's been every night. When you're not home I pray by covering you in the blood of Jesus."

"Thank you Ms. Daniels," I said hugging her.

"That's what I'm here for." She walked out and I lay down. I thought about Alonzo and then Julian until I cried myself to sleep.

That morning I arose from a dream that had become a constant for me so I would wake up feeling as if I had been with

Julian. Because of that dream my mornings were sad but I was full of joy. I decided to play some music that morning as I got dressed. I danced around my room thinking about the way Julian and I would dance the night away. When I stepped into the shower it was wet. I tried to remember what I did last night or if I had started sleep walking. Our favorite song came on so my thoughts quickly changed and I jumped in the shower singing as if I were singing to him, *"All my life I waited..."*

After my shower I quickly dressed and ran downstairs for breakfast so I could take Millie and JJ to school because this was going to be a special day. I had promised to take them out today for a special treat just the four of us. "Good morning Ms. Daniels," I announced as if I were singing.
"Well hello, you seem mighty chipper this morning."
"Yes I am and it's all thanks to you and our talk last night."
"What talk Alisha?" She asked looking puzzled.
"Mommy mommy," Millie and JJ yelled as they ran into my arms with AJ following close behind them. "Good morning babies."
"Mommy I'm not a baby. AJ is the baby because he has on a pull-up."

"No you're mommy's big boy but all of you together are my babies."

"Mommy, are you sad again?" Millie asked

"No Mille why would you think that?"

"You always get dramatic when you're sad." Ms. Daniels and I laughed "Little lady go eat your breakfast so we can leave."

"Good morning Alisha."

"Good morning Dad. I see you're getting ready to go play golf with Tommy."

"Yes and I'm going to school that young man again." He laughed.

"Well, have a good time and tell Tommy I said hi."

"Okay, I will see you in a few hours sweetie." He said as he kissed Ms. Daniels on the cheek. "Love you honey and I'll make lunch for you guys so come home after your game." Mr. Avery waved his hand and nodded in agreement as he walked out the door. Come on slow pokes it time for me and AJ to hang out while you guys go to school." She said. I grabbed a piece of toast and walked out the door with just as much excitement as the kids thinking about our ice cream and toy shopping day.

That evening after our shopping trip the kids played until it was bed time. AJ had fallen asleep first so we put him to bed without a bath. Millie wanted to stay up and play with her new dolls but JJ was sleepy and wanted to skip bath time; which was something he wanted to do every night. I allowed him to do it tonight because it was Friday and we were going to change the linen on Saturday. Millie stayed up an hour longer. The deal was she had to take a bath first, play in her room, and go to bed once the timer went off. After Millie got dressed for bed I sat in the backyard and fantasized about Julian knowing that it was time to let him go. "Hey Alisha, what are you doing back here?"

"I'm just thinking Tommy. What, are you doing over here?"

"Fighting again so instead of saying anything I just walk away."

"Tommy what are you guys going to do?"

"Alisha, I really don't know or care about what she's going to do but I'm getting a divorce and moving on with the kids."

"Tommy is that what you want?"

"Yes, Alisha I need some."

"Wait, pump your brakes. Why are you telling me this?"

"No not from you but...never mind."

"Are you cheating?"

"No but I want to."

"Please don't."

"I won't but I'm thinking about going home this weekend."

"What is there to think about?"

"I'm going without Isabella."

"Are you leaving the kids?"

"No, they're going with me but I'm nervous."

"Then why are you going home?"

"My dad has something to talk to me and Marcus about."

"He's not sick is he?"

"No or at least I don't think so but I'm a little nervous."

"Why?"

"Because my dad never calls me it's usually my mother. He might talk after she calls or I call him."

"Let's pray?" I said reaching for Tommy's hands.

"Yes and pray about these divorce papers I'm having written up."

"If that's what you want." After we prayed we talked for a while. We reminisced about Alonzo and the time we've had since he moved up here to be closer to me. Tommy put his arm around me and like old times we could feel each other's thoughts as we gazed into the night.

Regrets of Opportunity

There was a knock on my office door. Olivia answered to a big bouquet of pink and white roses. "Alisha I think it's for you," she yelled frantically causing me to run from the back with my gun in hand. What's wrong Olivia?"
"This man is delivering these to you."
"Why didn't you just take them?" I handed her the gun and motioned her to take it and put it up. "Thank you sir," I said. As I took the flowers the man behind the flowers said, "Alisha, how are you?"
"Mikael, is that you?
"Yes it is beautiful."
I rushed to put the flowers down and hugged him. "Oh my goodness, so when did you get back?"
"I got back last week and I tell you being on tour like that almost killed me."
"I'm so glad you're back but where's Faith and your son?"

"We split up and she moved back home with him while I was on tour." He walked in and sat down. "I didn't find out until my last two weeks of the tour. She had already been gone for six months before I knew anything."

I was a little shocked but selfishly I thought maybe we could make it work this time. He would be the perfect distraction. "So how are you taking it?"
"I'm working to keep me occupied because you can't force a person to be with you."
You're right about that." I laughed.
"Alisha we've had problems for years and I must say it was my fault."
"Oh really, you finally admit you were wrong or caused a problem."
"Alisha when I gave you up I became bitter and I despised Keira because of what she did."
"But Mikael you made the choice not her."
"If I had not been so consumed with being perfect for you our lives would've been different. I think this was perfect timing on her part because now we can see if it was meant for us to be together." Mikael stood up and leaned back some. "Hey pretty lady in the shoe string pants would you go on a date with me?"
I burst into laughter while trying to answer,

"Yes."

"Can I pick you up around seven and take you to dinner?"

"Yes, but where are you taking me?"

"It's a surprise."

"Okay see you at seven and you better not be late."

"Well pretty lady my name is Mikael Brats. I'm a trained dancer and comedian. What's your name?"

"I'm Alisha Coleman and I'm a general contractor and a student that's interning at a counseling center."

"Thank you because you made my day." He said kissing my hand.

"You didn't do that but it was nice meeting you." Mikael turned to walk out the door but turned before he opened it and said, "I'm serious."

"I know and I'll be ready."

As soon as he walked out the door I called Tommy. "Tommy, guess who just asked me out?"

"Alisha, why is it alright for you to do that but when we do it to you we get yelled at?"

"Tommy forgive me but I'm so excited."

"Who asked you out, because I'm scared to guess."

"Mikael, he's back for good and he wants to try us again."

"Wait, isn't he married?"

"No he never married Faith."

"So where is she?"

"They broke up six months ago."

"Are you sure you're not just a rebound?"

"Tommy this feels like déjà vu because you said the same thing the first time I met him." Tommy and I laughed. "I guess some things never change."

"Alisha, I think I'm going to cheat on Isabella."

"Wait, where did that come from?"

"She's been absent in our relationship for over a year now and I can't take it."

"Have you been seeing someone?"

"No but I'm attracted to another woman and I believe she feels the same way."

"Who is she and have you talked to her and does she know you're married; better yet do you?"

"I can't tell you and no we've never spoke about it and yes we both know I'm married."

"Please don't cheat on Isabella."

"Tell me why Clean-Up Woman." He laughed "Okay you're right but I know you and it's not in you."

"Alisha did you forget what almost happen six months ago."

"Well Tommy I had self-control and you had been drinking; which has been an issue for you lately."

"Cause it's been over a year and I need to have sex with my wife or move on." Tommy gave a sigh. We ended the night in silence.

That day I decided to focus on me so I called Ms. Daniels to let her know I was going to dinner with Mikael. After we talked I called Olivia into my office. "Yes Doc?"

"I wanted to ask you something."

"What's up?"

"Have you started dating yet?"

"What do you mean?"

"Have you gone out since you've been back?"

"Not with any guys."

"Why not?"

"I think I should leave men alone because all they do is hurt you."

"Are you saying you're a lesbian now?"

"Well girls treat me better and know how to please me."

"So you've gone that far or are you just reciting the straight woman's quote to satisfy their need to hide from the truth?" I motioned for her to sit next to me. "Olivia, if you're attracted to other women that's your choice but if you're doing it to hide from your pain it's not fair to you or the woman that falls for you."

She started crying, "Doc I can never go all

the way and she's frustrated with me but I just can't. I don't want to be with women."
"That's okay but you must be honest with her."
"I was and she said it was because of the way men hurt me so it's causing me to shut down in the bedroom."
"Olivia did you tell her you're not attracted to women?"
"No, I was scared I would hurt her."
"So what are you doing now?"
"Hurting her."
"I can't tell you what to do but you need to be honest with her."
"Can I take a few extra minutes for lunch and talk to her?"
"Yes." She ran out of the room dialing her phone.

When I got home at five Ms. Daniels was at the door and rushed me upstairs. "I've picked out some outfits for your date."
"Date, who's going on a date" Mr. Avery asked.
"I'm going on a date dad, with Mikael and he'll be here at seven." I said as I was running up the stairs. Millie was on my heels, "Mommy Mommy where are you going?"
"I'm going out to eat with an old friend."
"Good because we are ready for you to live

life."

"Millie what have I told you about repeating adult conversations or eavesdropping?"

"I know mommy but we are worried about you, because you're so young and have gone through so much."

"Milagro Vida Coleman-Avery if you don't stop I'm going to punish you."

"Yes mommy." Millie said as she eased out of my room. Ms. Daniels was in stitches.

"Ms. Daniels it's your fault, so I wouldn't be laughing so hard." I smiled.

"We have been concerned about you but we thought we were talking in code and spelling over her head but I guess not." She laughed.

"Once I jump in the shower I can get dressed." I said to her. I got in the shower while Ms. Daniels fussed with what I was going to wear. After I finished I put on lotion I put on my robe and picked out my outfit. "Ms. Daniels I need to look sexy."

"Okay but you've already caught his eye so I would do classy."

"Okay, show me what you have." The first three outfits made me look like I was going to church. "Okay Mama D I need classy sexy so I want to give him something to think about without showing him everything."

"Okay what about this." She handed me a

pink dress trimmed in white. A pair of pink and white flower patterned heels. Then I put on my pink and white pearl accessories. I quickly dressed and ran to look at myself in the full length mirror. "Mama D I think this is it."

"I agree Alisha and you look classy but sexy, so Mikael better watch out or he's hooked." We smiled as we looked in the mirror. I felt like I was in my twenty's again and I was on my first date with him. "Are you coming home tonight?"

"Yes Ms. Daniels I'm keeping them closed for real this time." We laughed as Mr. Avery bellowed from down stairs.

Mikael picked me up at seven on the dot and Mr. Avery questioned him as if I were his sixteen year old daughter. I walked down stairs and Mikael eyes lit up as he smiled at me. "Alisha you look beautiful and you match the flowers I have for you."

"Thank you Mikael," I said as I reached for the flowers.

"I'll take those." Ms. Daniels said as she came downstairs. "Mikael I would like for you to meet Alonzo's dad and stepmom, Mr. and Mrs. Avery."

"Hello," he said shaking their hands.

"Alisha I think it's time for us to go."

"Okay." I kissed Mr. Avery and hugged Ms. Daniels before I walked out.

We drove for about five minutes before Mikael broke the silence. "This is nice."
"Yes it is, so where are we going?"
"It's a surprise."
"Well your surprises are always remarkable." I smiled.
"That's because you are worth so much and deserve the best." I blushed as he squeezed my hand. Mikael pulled up to a building that looked abandoned but because of the lights and thumping from the music I knew it wasn't. I couldn't figure out why he would bring me to a place like this because it was not my kind of fun or atmosphere. Mikael blindfolded me after giving his keys to the valet. I was uncomfortable as we walked into the building. As we got onto the elevator and he rolled down the doors I said, "Mikael what are we doing?"
"What should've been done the first day I met you."
"What's that?" He pulled the doors open and took off my blindfold. I gasped at the beauty and felt like I was in my twenty's again. We were on our first date. Mikael got down on one knee and pulled out the ring I sent back while I was pregnant with Millie. "Alisha will you marry me?" I was stunned.

26

I also knew at that moment I was not in love with Mikael anymore but I didn't want to hurt him. I thought I could grow to love him again so I said, "Yes." He slipped the ring on my finger before he stood and lead me to our awaiting dance floor. "Mikael and I dance to our own beat as memories of the joy we once shared flowed through my mind.

After the dance we sat to enjoy the dinner he had his good friend Rafael a gourmet chef prepare. The waiter brought out Acaraje as we sipped on Brazilian Lemonade and reminisced. I wanted to ask about Faith but I knew it would spoil the moment. I became distracted when the main course arrived. The waiter placed Pao de Queijo in the center of the table before placing a bowl of Feijoada in front of both of us. I was lost in Mikael because I was stuck on the time we spent together before the break up and I wanted to relive that which I had lost. Mikael and I had made a life altering decision before the dessert, a Passion fruit pudding cake. Mikael decided to sell his house in two months and have our wedding in three. After dinner we danced once again before we departed and Mikael took me home.

Mr. Avery was sitting on the porch and cleared his throat before I reached the door. "Good evening dad."

"Alisha, are you sure you're ready to move on?"

"Dad, Alonzo has been gone for over a year so I think I am."

"I'm not talking about Alonzo I'm talking about Julian."

"Dad I'm okay." I was a little puzzled because he was concerned about my feelings for Julian instead of his son.

"Alisha," he said walking towards me. "I know what you had with Julian and it was a love I've never seen before it was almost super natural."

"I know because I can still feel him."

"I know baby, but you must let your dreams about him go and move forward."

I decided to change the subject. "I was on a date and you were sitting up waiting on me."

"I wasn't waiting but I was concerned because you keep playing it safe and you're going out with a man you know is unavailable or should I say won't notice your lack of emotions for him."

"Mr. Avery I'm engaged." I said holding my left hand up. He smiled as he looked at the ring and embraced me. While I was in his embrace he whispered, "That doesn't mean

a thing because you haven't let Julian go."
He kissed me on the cheek and walked into
the house. I sat on the porch and looked at
the stars because I knew he was right. I got
on my knees and prayed.

I walked in to Ms. Daniels asking
question as she followed me upstairs. "So
how did it go?"
"It was great and I got a ring too."
"Oh my let me get a closer look." She said
as she examined the ring. "So when's the
date?"
"In three months so I have a lot to do."
"Alisha didn't he just break up with
someone, so don't you want to slow down?"
"It will be alright."
"Alisha you're playing with fire."
"I know what I'm doing and it will be okay. I
slowly turned knowing she was right. "I
think I'm going to shower and go to bed it's
been a long day."

That night I went to bed with thoughts of
what I was going to do. I decided to write as
I prayed and thought about my life and the
revelation God was giving me at that
moment. I knew they were right but I
wanted the pain to stop. I was willing to
settle for something instead of nothing
because this was a great opportunity to
move forward.

Regrets of Illness

That day I received a call from a panicked Mike, "Alisha, Donna is being rushed to the hospital because she's having trouble breathing."

"Okay Mike I'll be there in twenty minutes." I ran into the other room, "Olivia, Donna's being rushed to the hospital so I have to go."

"Doc, Dawn is going to be here at ten to meet with you about the cake and they're bringing samples."

"Okay, tell her I rushed to the hospital to see about her aunt. Mikael will be here in a few minutes so tell him to choose." I rushed out the door before she could respond.

Mike and I sat at the hospital all night. Around one in the morning I could hear someone talking. When I opened my eyes Mike was on the phone talking to someone. I figured it was business. After he walked out I closed my eyes and fell asleep. Suddenly Julian appeared in my dreams, so we talked. I consoled him as his mother slept.

We knew Donna had given up because she was heartbroken about Julian's death so it was just a matter of time before she would pass from the illness that grief brings. A few hours later I could hear voices again and assumed it was Mike on his phone, so settled in and continued to sleep as the voices twirled in my head. "What are you doing here?"
"I came to see you."
"But that's impossible."
"No it's not the meds you're on that's making it possible."
"I've missed you." I heard Donna say as tears rolled down her cheeks. Then I heard her say, "Julian." I stood and couldn't believe my eyes. As tears flowed I sat down in disbelief. He walked over and embraced me. I couldn't tell if I was asleep or dreaming but I longed for this to be real.

Mike walked into the room, "Alisha," He startled me so I jumped up from the chair I had fallen asleep in. "Are you okay?" He asked.
"Yes, why do you ask?"
"You look as if you've seen a ghost."
"No, but I keep dreaming about one."

Richard walked in with more flowers. "Hello Alisha. Mike, how are you holding up?" He continued as he put the flowers on the table. "Has she opened her eyes yet?" "No, but everything is as it can be expected because she's my life." After I spoke and informed Mike I would be back later I walked out. As I walked towards the elevator I saw more of Donna's family but they didn't speak to me because they liked Rasheda better. They thought I stole Julian from her. I threw my hand up and spoke before I got onto the elevator.

Diving home I was thinking about Julian. The dreams I kept having at the hospital had to be happening because of my lack of sleep and the overwhelming desire to have him back. I dreaded going home because I was a mess and needed to get my head right before I got home. Tommy was out of town so I decided to go to the office and do some work. As I was driving to my office I remembered that I was engaged to Mikael until I remembered to call him about the cake. "Hey babe what's up I'm a little busy." He said instead of hello.
"I was just calling give me a call later."
"Okay class will be over in about twenty minutes." I hung up without saying anything.

When I pulled up I saw Olivia's car in the driveway. I thought why is she here. I decided to park down the street and call. "Hi Olivia are you still at the office because I thought I would stop by and get some work done."

"No I just," she paused. "Yes, I'm still here but I'm not alone or in your room."

"I know you're there but who are you with?"

"Deuces, I mean Charles Junior."

"Oh really," I laughed. "Well he's a great guy so I'll leave you guys alone." We hung up and I drove off.

I drove to a hotel when I realized that I hadn't talked to Tommy to find out what his father wanted. I pulled out my phone and called him. He answered before I pulled out of the parking lot at the hotel. "Hey Alisha I'm so glad you called."

"Tommy, are you okay?"

"Yes and no. Alisha, are you sitting down?"

"I'm driving so let me pull over." I pulled into a gas station. "What's wrong Tommy?"

"My mother has cancer but she's okay right now. She had her first treatment last week."

"What type of cancer?"

"Breast but my cousin has pancreatic cancer and he's at home waiting to die."

"Which cousin," I asked slowly.

"Elijah, you know the one that was

ordained after me."

"Oh my Lord, how is his wife and kids?"

"They're holding up pretty good. He got sick a few weeks ago and now he's about to die. This sucks because I haven't talked to him in two months. I told him I was divorcing Isabella so he read me the riot act since this was my second divorce."

"Tommy you know they don't believe in divorce down there, so what did you expect?"

"He was like a brother to me growing up but since I left the Church we haven't been as close."

"I know, but Tommy you can't beat yourself up about it."

"I'm not but his father doesn't want me around him so I've only seen him once and he didn't know I was there."

"Well you're going to have to find a way to find peace. How's everybody else?"

"Marcus asked about you when I picked him up from the airport."

"Wait picked him up where's Kashia?"

"I forgot to tell you she's eight months pregnant and they're expecting twins a boy and a girl."

"Well they said two and that's it. She didn't even tell me when we talked...dang that was almost six months ago."

"I know but they knew you were going

through a lot so they didn't want to hurt you."

"But it had been a while."

"Alisha you just said it yourself you haven't talked to her in six months but didn't even realize it had been so long."

"I know. I'm going to call her now. Tell Marcus I said hi and kiss your mom for me."

After I hung up I quickly called Kashia. She didn't even say hello but screamed, "Alisha, how are you?"

"No mama, how are you?"

"I'm sorry I didn't call you but..."

"That's neither here nor there so let's focus on you right now."

"I'm having twins and we've already picked out the names. The boy is going to be a junior and the girls name is Carmen or Ariel and well the middle name is still up in the air."

I'm happy for you, so are you okay?

"Yes, my mom flew in last week and refuses to leave until I have the twins."

"I guess we know whose family twins come from just kidding." I laugh

"I know you are because these are fraternal twins not identical."

"I'm going to let you go because I heard you were on bed rest so lay down and get some rest.

"I will Alisha, I'm so glad you called and are doing better."

"I am too. Love ya girl bye." When I finished talking to her I felt better and was already sitting in my driveway.

I walked in mouth first, "Ms. Daniels, guess who's having twins."

"I pray it's not you." Mr. Avery shouted from the family room.

"Don't pay him any attention. Who's having a baby?"

"Marcus and Kashia are having twins a boy and a girl."

"They knocked it out on the first try." We laughed.

"That's the good news. The bad and not so good is the fact the Tommy's cousin has pancreatic cancer and he's in hospice at home. His mom has breast cancer but they caught it early."

"Oh my thank God."

Mr. Avery yelled. "What are y'all doing in there we're ready for our dinner. Alisha wash your hands and help set the table."

"I guess he needs a swift kick in the rump" she laugh. We set the table as we talked about Tommy's family. After ten minutes we sat down for dinner. After dinner I watched a thirty minute show with the kids before I gave them a bath and tucked them in bed. Mr. Avery cleaned the kitchen and Ms. Daniels went downstairs to rest.

An hour later everyone was in the bed asleep except for me. I sat on the terrace when I remember that Mikael had not returned my call. I was doing everything in my power not to think about Julian but I lost that challenge again. I felt his tongue caress mine gently. As our passion mixed I exploded in lust. I pushed his gentle caresses between my legs. I moaned in pleasure as I remembered how much I missed him. Once Julian received the sweetness of my pleasure he picked me up and placed me on the bed. He locked the door. Julian returned to my warm embrace and eased his way into the moisture of his longing as if he wanted to savor each stroke while giving me a verbal delight with each movement. "Julian, I love you so much." I whispered as he held me tighter. Julian released his response to the pleasure he was experiencing. Julian collapsed beside me and pulled me closer as he whispered in my ear. His soothing voice caressed my ear as I fell asleep in his arms. I was in the perfect place.

I was awakened by my cell phone and couldn't find it. I searched in the dark and remembered I was on the terrace before I went to bed. I stumbled onto the terrace and pick up the phone. I searched my missed calls and saw that it was Mike. I dreaded returning that call because I figured Donna had passed. I felt guilty so I called back. "Alisha, I'm sorry if I woke you but I wanted to let you know about Malcolm."

I thought I really don't care unless he's dead. "What about him," I said.

"Malcolm is dead."

"What?"

"Yes you heard me he's dead."

Fully awake I asked, "How did he die?"

"He had an infection in his lungs. He didn't go to the hospital in time so he died. The good thing is he suffered and he deserved that for what he did to my son. I hated that man"

I had to change the subject because his joy was unsettling. "Dad how's mom?"

"She's sleeping right now but she wants to see you."

"I'll be there tomorrow morning."

"Okay baby girl get some sleep."

"I will see you tomorrow at nine."

"Okay, see you then." After we hung up I thought he called me baby girl, so I cried because I missed Julian.

After I got off the phone with Mike I thought about Malcolm and the way he suffered. My thoughts quickly focused on his family and their pain so I prayed. After praying I turned over and quickly fell asleep. I heard the bedroom door open so I jumped up, "Ms. Daniels is that you?"

"No babe it's me." He said locking the door behind him. I smiled as my husband walked over to me and kissed me on the forehead. "Where have you been baby I've needed you?"

"I had to go check on mother but she's better now so I came home to be with my wife."

"I've missed you," I caressed my husband's passion for me with gentle kisses until he couldn't control himself. As he enjoyed the warmth of my fully embraced kisses he relinquishing his appreciation for my ability to please him. Julian spread my legs until he found the sweet aroma that lured his tongue searching for its sweetness until he was satisfied. He caressed the softness of my passion as I pulled him closer and swiveled my hips until I released a scream of ultimate pleasure. "Julian," I screamed as I arched my back and squeezed my legs around his head. He couldn't stop enjoying the taste of the sweetness he caused to flow. I turned him over and slowly mounted the tip of my husband's throbbing manhood. With perfect balance I slowly circled the tip of his Julian throbbing desire for me. He grabbed me by the waist and thrust himself within me as if he had lost complete control. Julian flipped me over and continued his uncontrolled thrust until he couldn't hold his enjoyment and satisfaction of that moment. Julian held me in his arms again until we drifted off to sleep.

Ms. Daniels knocked on my bed room door at eight thirty before she called out. "Alisha, are you up yet?"
I answered searching for my phone because I had no idea of the time. "Yes but what time is it?"
"It's almost eight thirty and the kids have already left for school are you alright?"
"Yes." I said as I opened the door.
"Are you sure I heard you talking last night but I realized you were praying and the door was locked so I went back down stairs."
"I was talking to Mike and he told me Malcolm had died so I prayed for his family."
"Where was he?"
"Somewhere in the Midwest I guess Lealtà hid him until he got so sick they had to

take him to the hospital where he died."

"What happen to him?"

"It was a lung infection you know after he was shot he kept getting sick."

"So they're still not going to charge her with anything?"

"No she was supposed to be in witness protection for her testimony, which in my opinion wasn't enough to drop all the charges. Hopefully they will charge her for hiding him all this time."

"That's not right but it's the law, so we have to pray and find a way to change it."

"You're right and Mike is working on that but my case is irrelevant because it's over so hopefully it will help others."

"I'm sure it will."

"I need to get up so I can visit Donna."

"Have they said when she's going home?"

"I'm not sure," suddenly I remembered what Julian told me in my dreams. "I think she's doing better or at least I hope so because she's been so heartbroken about Julian."

"Losing a child can do that to you because it's just not right to bury your child and you're still here living life." After she said that Ms. Daniels walked out without saying a word. I couldn't imagine that feeling so I took a shower and thanked God for being a mother to three healthy children and peace for the unborn babies I lost.

When I arrived at the hospital around nine thirty Donna was up and walking around. "Good morning Donna."
"Hello Alisha."
"I'm glad you're out of bed. That means you must be feeling better?"
"Yes, I must say that I am." She said as she fiddled with her flowers and cards "Where's Mike?"
"He went to get my clothes so I could leave today."
"You're leaving today?"
"Yes and I wanted to wear my favorite pants suit home to celebrate my new found joy and my secret."
"Secret, what kind of secret?"
"I can't tell you." She said looking around as she motioned for me to come closer.
"Julian is alive but like that evil man's wife he's in witness protection until they catch all the bad guys."
I knew she was talking about Malcolm but I also knew that Julian was...I thought about the realness of my dreams and thought maybe he was alive and I wasn't dreaming.
"What makes you think that Donna?"
"I saw him yesterday he tried to wake you up but you never did open your eyes."
"Donna, are you..."
"Good morning Alisha. Donna, here are the clothes you asked for." Mike interrupted us

as he walked in. Donna grabbed her clothes and ran off to the bath room to change. "I can tell by the puzzled look on your face she told you the secret about Julian."

"Is it true?" I asked hoping it was true.

"No, my wife is on so many drugs she thinks its twenty years ago."

"Mike, what are you going to do?"

"Nothing she'll forget about it in a few days."

"I hope she doesn't sink into a depression worse than what she went through."

"Alisha, my wife is strong so I think she'll be able to handle it. How are you holding up after all the info you've received?"

"This too shall pass, so I'll survive." The nurse walked in with transport and a cart to carry everything out. Mike walked out so he could pull the car around. I gathered everything and placed it on the cart. Donna walked out of the bath room and sat in the wheel chair.

On my way home Tommy called to let me know his cousin passed last night. His Uncle had a change of heart so Tommy was at his cousin's bedside when he took his last breath.

Regrets of A First

I awake that Saturday morning ready for Tonya's big day. We rented the large cottage at Greyfield Inn, which is located on the coast of Georgia. We slept four or two to a room so the six bedrooms were full. When I awake I saw that I had a text from Mikael. We decided to postpone the wedding yet again but this time because of his upcoming tour. For the past few months we texted more than we talked. I knew it was time to let him go but I didn't know how.

"Alisha, why are you looking so worried I'm the one getting married?"

"Was I, please forgive me Tonya."

"No problem but what's wrong?"

"This is your day and it's all about you."

"Yes it is and I want to know what's bothering you."

"It's Mikael I know I don't want to marry him and I think he should work it out with Faith but..."

"But what, girl call him and tell him the truth."

"I don't want to hurt him."

"Which one do you think is worse, Alisha? It's time to put your emotional needs first.

Every since I met you you've put everyone else's feelings ahead of yours and consumed yourself with temporary satisfaction which doesn't last long. You had that with Julian but it's time to let him go and find your peace." I wanted to tell her about the Julian dreams but was ashamed, so I walked off. I pulled out my phone and called Mikael instead. The call went to voice mail so I left him a message.

When I walked into the room Renee and Tamika had joined Tonya. "Hello ladies are you ready to support our girl for her big day?"
"Yes yes and I have the make-up bag charged and ready. Renee turned towards me and said, "Oh by the way Alisha you are going to wear make-up today."
"If she doesn't want to wear it then don't force her." Tamika chimed in.
"This is my day and I don't want her to upstage me by looking good without make-up." Tonya jokingly exclaimed. We all laughed
"I'll get our breakfast and bring it up."
"Wait didn't you hire someone to do that?"
"Yes, to cook not serve." I said as I walked downstairs.

I walked into the kitchen and Karl was already preparing breakfast for Lamar's parents. "Good morning." I said as I walked over to Karl and handed him our breakfast order. The parents nodded as I walked out onto the porch with my juice. After I sat down my cell phone rang, "Hi Mikael."

"Hey Alisha you sounded strange on the message what's up?"

"Mikael I think we need to talk face to face so I was calling because I wanted to fly out to see you after I leave here."

"No, I mean don't baby. Please don't come."

"Mikael is everything alright?"

"Yes but Faith is coming so we can make final arrangements on child support and visitation."

"Mikael I'm going to ask you something and regardless of how you think I'll feel I want the truth."

"Yes Alisha and I know you're not in love with me but you love me enough to sacrifice for me." Mikael cleared his throat, "Thanks for being my friend so I'm still going to marry you." He laughed.

"Mikael I'll call you when I leave tomorrow."

After we hung up I walked around the cottage. I saw a man in the distance that was eye catching so I quickly turned and bumped into another guest. "Excuse me I didn't see you there."

"Alisha," he said looking surprised.

"Rodney Mitchell what are you doing here?"
"My daughter wants to have her wedding here so Nichole and I came with her to check it out."
"Congratulations, so how is your son?"
"He was killed by a drunk driver after he got his first car."
"I'm so sorry to hear that."
"So what are you doing here?"
"My friend is getting married and I'm the maid of honor because she couldn't choose between her two best friends, so to keep down confusion she picked me." We laughed. He grabbed my left hand, "I see you're engaged or is it married?"
"No engaged to the guy that always sent me those flowers."
"Really, that guy is just now proposing to you."
"Yes."
"Wait, you don't seem to be excited about it."
I quickly changed the subject. I realized he was still holding my hand so I slowly pulled my hand back and said, "So where's your wife?"
"Nichole and my daughter are still asleep so I decided to take a walk before we got the grand tour."
"Well Rodney, it was nice seeing you again."
"Yes it is yes it is." He said smiling. As we

turned and walked towards our destinations he turn and asked, "Is your number the same?"

"Yes and I still have the same house." He smiled as he walked off. I wanted to kick myself after I gave him so much information but it was okay because he was still married and I was engaged so cheating would not be a concern.

When I walked into the kitchen Karl was fussing, "Where have you been the food is ready and the bride should not have a cold breakfast."

"Forgive me Karl."

"Good Morning sunshine," Andrew said as I turned to walk out. I ran over to give him, Angela, and Tonya's parents a hug. "Let me take this breakfast upstairs to the girls and I'll talk to you guys later." I ran upstairs and almost ran into Mark, Lamar's brother and best man. "Slow down pretty lady, I wouldn't want you to hurt yourself but if you did I would be willing to carry you every step of the way." He smiled.

"Thanks but I'm engaged." He had been trying to hit on me since I met him and I wasn't nice at all. "Well if you let me hit it I could knock the frost off of it and you wouldn't be so cold." I ignored him and continued upstairs.

When I opened the door all I could hear was crying. "I'm sorry for taking so long but here's breakfast." I said sitting the food down. "Alisha, its Renee she's crying because she thinks she'll be alone now." Tamika said as Tonya comforted her. I kneeled in front of Renee and lifted her head by her chin. "Renee this is life and we all have to face it good or bad but we decide that with our choices. You decided to be alone but you're not because God is always there and so are your friends but you need to allow yourself to have that special someone in your life."

"Alisha I want to but I'm scared."

"I know but in your fear you have to take one step and before you know it you've conquered that fear."

"Try it with Joe he's been into you since he met you." Tamika blurted.

"You mean that cutie that's walking down the aisle with her?" I said.

"Yes, he's really sweet and a nice guy." Tonya turned to me. "Girl he's a widow and was raising his kids before he married his deceased wife."

"Wait did he have kids before or after he was married and how is he a widow if he was raising the kids alone?" I asked because I didn't know him like they did.

"He had two children by this woman that

decided to walk out on him one day. He met Kimberly and they got married after two months of dating. They had been together for ten years when she died last year. He hasn't looked at another woman until he met Renee two months ago."

"Renee there you have it. I had to check myself because I saw him this morning and all I can say is if I were you I would be dating him." I laughed which cause everyone to laugh. We continued to talk as we ate and continued until the knock on the door reminded us it was time to get dressed. "Why are you ladies still sitting around when the ceremony starts in less than forty-five minutes?" Angela barked. We jumped up and got dressed. They had already taken our showers so I jumped in while they dressed. We were dressed and ready to go in thirty minutes.

The groom's parents Charlotte and Clarence walked first, then the bridesmaids, the flower girl and then the ring bearer. The bride was escorted down the aisle by her father Andrew as the traditional music played and everyone stood. Lamar was smiling so hard I thought his face was going to break and Tonya was trying to hold back tears because she said she wouldn't cry. The outdoor ceremony was beautiful and flawless. We had to take pictures before we could go to the reception and I was so hungry my stomach started to growl because I didn't eat breakfast. Tonya started picking at me because my stomach was making so much noise. After the pictures of the wedding party and parents were done I rushed to the buffet. While in line I saw Rodney again, "Hey stranger so we meet again." He said.

"Yes but what are you doing here?"

"I was invited by the groom we went to school together so when he saw me and found out why I was here he invited me to come to the reception." As we were talking his daughter walked up, "Daddy did you get the sauce that comes with the meat?" He quickly introduced us. "Chrissie I would like you to meet Alisha." She turned up her nose and said, "Hi." Before walking off Rodney nervously said "Forgive me but she's become a little mean since..." He was suddenly distracted "I have to go I'll call you soon." I thought I hope not but brushed it off and focused on my plate. As I ate I could see Tonya pointing at me because I was sitting with the guest instead of the wedding party. I laughed and walked up to sit with the wedding party before they started the speeches. When I sat down my eyes immediately fell on Rodney so I quickly averted my eyes. Renee whispered, "I think you have an admirer."

"I'm engaged so I can't go there."

"I can respect that but he doesn't seem to care." She said.

In my head I screamed Lord why is this happening to me I am beginning to lust this man and I'm engaged to Mikael. Lord, help me with my lustful ways. I leaned over to Tonya and said I'm not feeling well so I'm going to go to the room for a little while."

"Okay but we're going to cut the cake in ten minutes do you think you can stay long enough for that?"

"Yes for you I'll do it." I knew my stomach was fine but the area between my legs was steaming for Rodney and I couldn't understand why. I knew the danger of being with a married man and I was engaged to Mikael so I was not supposed to feel this way. "So who is he?" Tonya whispered.

Her question startled me and pulled me away from my thoughts, "What?"

"That fine piece of man that won't take his eyes off of you sitting on our left, I think Lamar knows him."

"That's Rodney I met him after I bought my first house and he wanted me to do some work for him, which doesn't matter because I'm engaged remember."

"Well it looks as if he wants you to do

another job."

"Well that's disrespectful because that's his wife and daughter sitting with him."

"You must have had some kind of impression because he doesn't seem to care." She leaded over and whispered something to Lamar before she returned to our conversation. "Alisha, Lamar just said he's…" Lamar snatched her up so they could dance. He loved dancing but Tonya could do without it. After they danced and the floor was open for us to dance Lamar danced with me until Tonya eased between us and switched partners. I turned around to see Rodney smiling and my panties filled with desire as he embraced me. Tonya was smiling and encouraging me as he swayed to the music with me. "Where's your wife and daughter." I asked looking for an escape. "Nichole had a headache so my daughter took her back to the room."

"Don't you think you should go check on her?"

"She'll be alright she has our daughter with her and Jonathan is on the way."

"Okay, I guess we can enjoy this moment." We continued to dance until they cut the cake that was supposed to be cut over an hour ago.

After we got our cake we walked to the lake and sat on a swing and talked. "So how's the construction business going?"
"I stopped dealing with the day to day aspects of it, so I'm thinking about selling my half out completely but without letting Charles talk me out of it again. So what about you did you move up in the company?"
"No, I'm going to retire in two years because I'm the Pastor of New Life Missionary Church."
"Really, so how long have you been the Pastor?"
About two years but God allowed me to start the ministry five years ago with bible study and mission trips. Obedience causes us to grow so we have over two thousand members nationwide."
"I'm so happy for you."
"So are you still counseling?"
"No, I opened a community center and oversee the daily activities which include counseling. I married a wealthy man that wanted me at home with the kids but when he died I threw myself back into the swing of things."
"So you have kids and you're engaged but do you have peace?"
"Rodney I'm saved and I'm very active in Church my best friend was a Pastor,

Tommy remember. That reminds me he's getting ordained in our Church next week."

"But what about you have you answered your call?"

"No, I haven't but I know what it is."

"What about your fiancé is he saved and walking with God?"

"Yes, but he struggles with the understanding of spirituality."

"Really, so is he ready to be the head of the household when you're the one with the money?"

"He has money he's Mikael Brats the comedian and radio personality."

"You're engaged to him?"

"Yes."

"How did you, oh yeah you met before he was famous but I though he was married."

"No, he and Faith had a spiritual marriage."

"A what," he asked looking puzzled.

"Don't ask but it was what they wanted to do before the birth of their son."

"Be careful Alisha."

"That's why I am having second thoughts and I've changed the wedding date twice."

"Why are you having second thoughts?"

"I'm not in love with him and I think he needs to try to work it out with Faith."

"So are you having sex?"

"No, I decided after my second husband died to wait until I was married."

"Wait, you had two husbands to die?"

"Yes, they were killed by jealous lovers."

"Alisha, are you still dating married men?"

"No I learned my lesson."

"So you can see your self-worth now?"

"Yes and I'm waiting for marriage."

"That's great because before I answered my call I was sleeping with everything that was beautiful and opened her legs."

"That's hard to believe."

"Well life allows you to make different choices according to circumstances and I chose the wrong way to handle..." Suddenly his phone rang, "Hello. I have to go my daughter is upset." We hugged and he said, "Come visit the Church soon." Rodney Mitchell ran off and my desire followed. I looked at my watch and realized I needed to get my things together so I could go see Mikael.

Rodney Mitchell was the first husband I slept with and looking at him and his wife today parts of me regretted that decision to allow my lustful passion overrule my senses. After talking with him I was glad I kept my desires to myself.

Regrets of Divorce

I arrived at the airport five minutes before they started boarding so I had to make a mad dash to my gate. I knew Mikael left me a key at the front desk just in case I had a break in my schedule and could fly out. My four hour trip was pleasant and I arrived at one o'clock in the morning. I took a cab to the hotel and I went to the front desk to get my key. I walked to the elevators thinking about Rodney and sighed. I erased those thoughts when the doors opened to the eighth floor. I walked to room 812 and opened the door to his room.

At home Isabella and Tommy were fighting after it was revealed that she had an abortion. Tommy found a letter from the insurance company because she filled out the paperwork wrong. "Isabella was this the first abortion you've had?"
"Thomas this is my body not yours so I can do whatever I want."

"We are married so I deserve a conversation or a vote."

"Tommy that won't happen because I'm not your wife you treat me like a slave."

"Isabella, please tell me how I mistreat you?"

"Thomas you won't let me go back to school."

"Isabella that's a lie I got you a tutor and you fired her."

"She was flirting with you and I wasn't going to deal with that."

"Isabella that woman wasn't thinking about me you really need to get over your insecurities."

"I hate you Thomas." She said storming off. Suddenly she paused and said, "Did you have sex with Alisha?"

"What are you talking about I've been faithful to you since day one."

"Are you in love with her?"

"Isabella, I'm in love with you you're the only woman for me"

"I asked if you were in love with Alisha?"

"Where is this coming from?"

"I found this letter." She handed him a letter from Ma Carrie telling my grandmother to pray for our relationship. Tommy looked at her and said, "She was talking about our friendship because of my wife."

"But, it doesn't matter because I'm not on your bank accounts." Isabella stormed out of the room and Tommy went to my house.

The suite was dark when I walked in so I eased into the bedroom and to my surprise Mikael was not alone. I eased out of the bedroom and sat on the sofa. I had fallen asleep and was awaken by a noise around six so I sat up. Mikael walked out of the room, "Good morning Mikael." I said startling him.

"Baby, what are you doing here?" He said looking nervous.

"I flew in late last night to be with you."

"But you were supposed to call me before you left."

"Why, so you could get her out of your bed before I got here?"

"Alisha, it's not what you think she was tired so she crashed here but nothing happened."

"Well open the door back up and let's see if she's naked like you."

He looked down and attempted to plead his case, "Alisha I..."

Faith walked out the room with his shirt on, "Look Mikael and I are getting back together so you can get out because you are interrupting our reunion."

"Faith, that's fine but I need Mikael to tell

me that."

Mikael turned towards her, "Faith I left Alisha a keycard at the front desk so…"

"So you knew she was coming, did you tell her I was spending the weekend with you?" I sat back and watched this deja vu moment and stretched out on the sofa, "Wake me in an hour so I can catch my flight."

"You can't stay here Alisha." Faith yelled as Mikael pushed her back into the room. Mikael came back out in less than five minutes. "Alisha I'm sorry," he whispered as he sat down next to me. "I haven't been with a woman in over six months so I slept with her…"

I cut him off, "Mikael you are still in love with her and I think you should work it out so if putting me out will help you then do it. I'll still love you and be your fiend."

"Alisha she's jealous of you and has been since day one and…" Faith stormed out of the room with her bags. "Mikael you knew I was coming to work on our relationship so you have a choice it's either me or her."

"I'll leave Mikael because I didn't call first, so I'll crash at the airport."

"No Alisha he needs to choose."

"Faith we're not some cheap prize to be picked over. We are ladies and one of us should concede and I concede because clearly Mikael loves you." I thought this is my way out. "I'm leaving please forgive me for interrupting your reunion." Mikael winked at me as Faith stormed back into the bedroom. When I opened the door Kerri was about to knock on the door so we were both startled. "Alisha, what are you doing here?"

"Mikael and I had plans but I didn't know he had plans with Faith as well, so could you discreetly give this to him." I handed her the ring and walked towards the elevator.

When I got home I went in my room with the thought of sleeping for two days but I knew my thoughts were just a dream when Tommy walked into the room. "Alisha, Isabella has been gone for a week so I filed for divorce because she abandoned us and I don't know where she is."

"Tommy I thought you filed for divorce less than a month ago?"

"I did but she wanted to go to counseling after she signed the papers."

"What happen?"

"I don't know," Tommy walked over and lay down next to me. "Alisha, are you okay?"

"Yes why would you ask me that?"

"Your engagement ring is gone."

"Mikael and I called off the wedding."

"Well since you changed the date twice I knew you didn't want to get married, but what happen?"

"I found him in bed with Faith."

"I'm sure he said it's been awhile since I've been with a woman."

"Yes, he did." I laughed.

"Classic Mikael." He laughed, "So how was the wedding?"

"It was great but I saw Rodney Mitchell there..."

"Wait isn't he the first married man you slept with and wanted almost as much as you wanted Julian?"

"Yes but he's still unavailable and a Pastor so I can't touch him."

"But if he was available you would?"

"No, because I'm not touching anyone sexually except my husband."

"I'm proud of you but I have a confession to make."

"What is it Tommy?"

"Isabella thinks I'm sleeping with you but it was Naomi that I almost slipped with." I jumped up oh my god I knew it and you said no but I called it when you met her."

"Calm down Alisha I'm not done." I lay back down next to him. "We've been talking for a couple of days but decided to stop until my divorce was final and then we are going to get married."

"Should I plan the secret wedding or is it going to be a job for Dawn?"

"No we are going to have a small intimate union at the church in sixty days."

"Okay I get it the divorce is final in thirty days you date for a month and then get married.

"Alisha, she cleaned out her account left the kids at your house and disappeared. I pray she doesn't come back." Tommy sat up quickly, "Alisha, she did sign the first set of divorce papers," Tommy jumped up and ran out the room.

After Tommy ran out of the room my phone rang I didn't want to answer it because I didn't know the number but they called again, "Hello."

"Hi Alisha, this is Rodney."

"Hi Rodney, how are you?"

"I'm great, so how was your trip home?"

"It was a little rocky because I went to see Mikael when I left Saturday and gave him the ring back."

"So you're not obligated anymore."

"I guess not, how was your trip and is your wife better?"

"It was nice I just got home today but Nichole went home with Jonathan her husband." I thought did he just say what I think he said, "Who?"

"Yes, I'm divorced." He paused, "I know I never got a chance to tell you we were divorced because we kept getting interrupted."

"So, how long have you been divorced" I asked.

"Six years and I've been looking for my first lady for the past two years. Two months ago I met Rebecca."

"I'm still in shock about the fact you're divorced."

"Well before I started cheating with you she had been cheating on me with Jonathan. I guess that would explain the last minute trips. Jonathan was married with kids so they broke up. I caught her in the bed with Jonathan again and I think we would've made it work but my son, Dalton, was there and he saw the whole thing. He jumped in his car and drove off. Within minutes he was hit head on by a drunk driver and killed. After he passed I started sleeping with women at our church and in our circle for almost two years. One day I woke up next to a woman that was my daughters best friend's mom and I knew then I had to stop."

"My goodness I..."

"Don't worry about it because it was divine intervention that I saw you this weekend."

"I believe so."

"So would you be willing to go to dinner with me tonight?"

"I have to check my schedule because I haven't seen the kids in almost a week."

"Well I can respect that. Call me later so we can talk and catch up."

"Okay Rodney." After I hung up I thought about the events of my weekend before I got up to take a shower and check on the kids.

I walked downstairs to greet AJ because he was the only one at home. "Good morning Ms. Daniels."

"Good morning lady I thought you would be gone until Wednesday."

"I did too but Mikael and I broke up."

"So you finally told him you didn't want to get married?"

"No, I didn't and why is everyone saying that?"

"Well it must be the people that know you because you kept changing the date and you were not in love with him."

"I can't argue with you but I tried to fall in love with him."

"Alisha, stop trying to force God's hand."

"I'm not Mikael was supposed to be my husband."

"Was he, maybe God used him to open your mind or vise verse?"

"Well he's with Faith and I'm glad because I

couldn't take it anymore."

"What being with a man you don't want to marry because y'all are both in love with someone else?"

"I guess so Mama D." we laughed as I walked into the family room to see AJ. He jumped up screaming, "Mommy."

"Hey big man, how are you?"

"Good, now sit down and watch TV." I sat down and realized Ms. Daniels was making breakfast alone. "Ms. Daniels where's dad?"

"He took the kids to school."

"I thought Ms. Pye did that."

"She did before Isabella ran off now she watches Thomas' little ones."

"I didn't know."

"Thomas is working from home until next week or until he finds a full time live in nanny."

"Well, I'm back so I can help."

"He asked if my daughter was available since she lost her job but he might not want her to live there with her kids."

"I'm sure he wouldn't mind. Have you asked her yet?"

"No, she's coming over later after a job interview and I will ask her then." I laughed as I thought about what Tommy said.

"Alisha, you think Thomas is sweet on my Naomi?"

"Ms. D I think they are sweet on each other

and I think they would make a great couple."

"Well I don't think she is because she's always avoiding him and…"

"It just hit you huh?"

"I didn't even notice, is that why Isabella left was he having an affair with my daughter?"

"No, they've never had sex but the first day they met it was like an instant attraction."

"Whew that's good to know but when did they meet?"

"Your engagement party was the first time they met."

"That long so they've been holding it together for all these years."

"Yes and I must say I respect that."

"Well now I hope Isabella doesn't come back because my baby deserves a good man like Thomas."

"He deserves to be happy so I pray your daughter is the one for him."

"Alisha, I just need to know one thing because I know after Alonzo passed Thomas would spend the night with you and I know what Carrie would say about you two but I saw him coming down stairs this morning, so I have to know are you and Thomas sleeping together?"

"No we are not! I know it's hard for people to see our relationship and the closeness we share and not think it's more than what it is but we've been together since we were born so we have a strong bond."

"I just believe that the wife should be her husband's best friend."

"I agree but we will always be friends no matter what."

"Well I don't want my daughter to get mixed up in some mess and get hurt."

"That's very hypocritical of you because if you feel that way about a man and woman than you should've spoke up when Tommy was with Isabella."

"Alisha I can't believe you."

"Well Ms. Daniels I can't believe you because you know me and you know Tommy, so you know we've never had that type of relationship."

"Well Alonzo was uncomfortable with it and lately so was Isabella."

"Alonzo was always insecure and Isabella was probably cheating herself the reason she felt that way but however you felt before your daughter came into the picture is the way you should feel now."

"Okay Alisha you're right, forgive me."

I walked out of the kitchen and sat down to continue watching TV with AJ while Ms. Daniels continued doing whatever she was doing in the kitchen.

When Mr. Avery came in he could tell something was wrong with her as he walked into the kitchen, "Baby is everything alright?"

"Yes honey, I'm just getting some things together for dinner tonight."

"Alisha, is that you in there?"

"Yes sir."

"Are you going to tell me what's going on."

"I'm not sure what you're talking about Dad."

"There's an eerie feeling in this house and I don't like it."

"Alisha called me a hypocrite," Ms. Daniels blurted.

"Alisha, now why would you do a thing like that?"

"Ask your wife."

"Baby, why did she say something like that to you," he asked.

"I asked her if she was sleeping with Thomas after I realized my daughter likes him."

"Why would you ask her something like that?"

"Well Alonzo said their relationship made him uncomfortable."

"Sarah you know my son was insecure and I told him that when he came to us about their relationship."

"But Isabella said it too and after Alonzo

died he would spend the night here."

"Sarah I can't believe you now you know you thought Isabella was messing around on Thomas and Carrie told you those two would sleep in the same bed and they had been doing it for years when one of them was hurting."

"Well I don't want him doing that with my daughter because a wife should be her husband's best friend."

"Then why didn't you say anything while he was with Isabella?"

"Because she's not my daughter and she deserved what she got because of the last baby."

"Ms. Daniels I would never hurt your daughter but I'm not going to change how I treat Tommy just because you're uncomfortable."

"Alisha your feelings are not the only ones you need to consider."

"Ms. Daniels I can tell you this if Tommy or his wife has an issue I will respect that because it's about them not you or me."

"Alisha where is this meanness coming from what did I do to you?"

"Honey she's telling you the truth and you don't want to face it."

"I can't believe it you're turning on me for her, your ex-wife was right Alisha has some kind of a spell on all of you." She ran out of the room crying and he followed her.

After lunch I put AJ down for his nap and walked out onto the terrace. Naomi came over later. Ms. Daniels left out with her after a few minutes. I was annoyed with her because she was making a mountain out of a mole hill. I was trying to workout but my mind was on Ms. Daniels. My phone rang so I was distracted by Mikael's call.
"Hi Mikael is everything alright?"
"Yes I just called to invite you to our wedding in two weeks."
"Is it another spiritual thing or are you going to get married for real this time?"
"For real when I get home, so I'll send you an invite."
"Congratulations I'm happy for the two of you."
"Are you sure you're okay with it?"
"Yes Mikael I wanted to break it off but I didn't know how so now you can marry the woman you love."
"Thanks for being a good friend Alisha."
"That's what I'm here for." We hung up with an understanding and respect for each other. The only issue was the fact I was alone again and had to face life without that special someone.

I texted Rodney earlier that day to let him know I would not be available for dinner tonight. I picked Millie and Julian up from school to their surprise. As Millie got into the car she said, "Mommy you're not supposed to be at home yet."

"I know baby but my plans changed."

"I'm glad you're home because I missed you," Julian said.

"Well I missed all three of you." I smiled as I looked at them in the rear view mirror, "Would you like to go out and eat or go home?"

"I want to see Uncle Jerri." Millie screamed. I called Jerri to let him know we were on our way to Jack's because Millie wanted to see him. Once we arrived Jack met us at the door and let me know Jerri was on the way. He sat us in a private dining area.

Jerri was there five minutes after we were seated. "Hi kids, I'm a little late."

"We just sat down so that's okay."

"Sit next to me Uncle Jerri." Millie exclaimed. "I will darling." Jerri rushed over to Millie. "I'm starving so what looks good to you?"

"I'm having the sirloin with potatoes and the grilled asparagus." Millie sang.

"Alisha that confirms she's yours. I've never met an elementary school child that could order with such elegance." Jerri turned to the boys and what would you gentlemen like. AJ yelled, "Mac and chees, green beans with garlic butter and meat." Jerri and I smiled. "I will have the parmesan encrusted fish with the vegetable medley and garlic mashed potatoes." JJ announced. "Alisha I must say you need to cook more and stop eating out so these kids can appreciate normal food."

"I do they eat pizza, hotdogs and burgers all the time."

"We just enjoy a fine cuisine from time to time plus Uncle Jack doesn't sell hamburgers." Millie announced.

"Well I guess Little Miss Millie read me," Jerri laughed. We placed our orders and enjoyed our meal. Jack pop in the room from time to time and join in on the conversation.

Regrets of Lost Hope

I went to bed early that day because I was sick but was awaken by a ranting Tommy. I screamed after he startled me, "Tommy, what's wrong?"

"Thomas I told you that girl was sick now get out of here." Ms. Daniels commanded.

"It's alright Ms. Daniels."

"Alisha would you like something to eat?"

"No, but I know you're going to make me eat anyway." She laughed as she walked out the door, "You know me well. I'll be back with something light for you to eat." I turned my attention back to him. "Tommy what's wrong?"

"Alisha I'm free my divorce is final."

"Tommy I'm happy for you."

"Alisha I'm going to call Naomi so we can go out."

"I figured that would be the first thing you did."

"Well I had to talk to you about it first, so

what do you think..."

"Tommy you're divorced, so do what's best for you and the kids."

"The kids miss Isabella?"

"So, what are you supposed to do if you don't even know where she is?"

"I have an idea."

"An idea of what," I asked.

"Of where she went.

"Where did she go?"

"She went back home."

"How do you know?"

"I got a detailed copy of her last phone bill from a cell phone I knew nothing about."

"A cell phone how long did she have it?"

About two years and most of the calls were to her parents," he lied.

"So have you called her parents?"

"I called them the week she disappeared but they said they hadn't heard from her in days. I knew they were lying because she's been calling home a lot over the past two years and it increased each month until the day she cleaned out her bank account and disappeared."

"Are you sure this is what you want to do?"

"Yes Alisha it's already done." We hugged before he departed.

Ms. Daniels walked in with a tray, "Where's Tommy Alisha?"

"He decided to celebrate his divorce."
"What divorce?"
"His got the final papers in the mail today."
"I thought he had to wait until he put a notice in the paper and all that other stuff."
"He had forgotten she signed the divorce papers that he gave her the first time."
"So who is he going to celebrate with?"
"He didn't tell me that part."
"Is he going out with my daughter?"
"I don't know who he's going out with or where but you can call Naomi and ask her."
"They are grown so I'm not going to interfere." She walked out of the room. I could tell she was upset. At that moment I was glad the kids were at Mike and Donna's for the week.

I took my food out onto the terrace and pondered my life and realized I was not alone. I knew it was not because I had kids, Tommy, Ms. Daniels or my in-laws. I was not alone or lonely because God is always with me. I just desired to have a companion and was going about it the wrong way. After I finished eating I lay back and begun to journal as I pondered why I thought I was alone. Grams and Papa were always there for me but when my mom died I was crushed and desired to know more about her and my father. I never knew my father so the time I spent with Charles and other older men was my father figure comfort. My best and closest friend was a man. I always had a fear of getting too close to females because of that summer day. I never told anyone who the girl was that ran off that day because before Tommy and I became close she was my best friend except on Wednesday's that's when Tommy and I would go fishing and tadpole hunting, which something we did every summer because we had the lake to ourselves. I spent time with her at her house doing stupid girl stuff and we had sleep overs but as we got older we grew further apart because I was a tomboy and she was a girlie girl. She desired to be a part of the popular crowd and started hanging around them as a flunky. She did whatever Lisa told her to do but she didn't know that I was Lisa's target that summer day. After she moved away Grams kept in touch with her mother but Emily would never be the same again. After they moved she didn't talk for a year and she had a nervous breakdown a year later she was never the same again.

When Tommy and I took our summer trip before college we went to see her but she was not the same person. During our first year in college she committed suicide after she sent letters out telling of the event that summer day. The town was in an uproar because I wasn't the only girl they had raped. The sheriff and the Mayor were voted out of office. The sheriff moved to the outskirts of town and the Mayor retired and they moved to the city with his wife's widowed sister. The boys never came back to town except to visit after they were sent off. Two of the boys are doing well. I kept up with them until my second year in college and sent them reminders every year on that day of what they had done.

I held on to that day because I lost my self-worth and all hope for a future. After Mikael left and Terrance broke me I never regain the importance of who I was but I put up a good front. I needed the relationship I had with Tommy because it reminded me of the innocence and purity I had before I became this pleasure consuming monster that craved some kind of sick power and control as I pleased men causing them to become weak. I knew there were only a few men in my life that really loved me for me because every other man I was with only lusted for me and they were a temporary satisfaction for my need to feel powerful not realizing I was becoming powerless. Mikael loved me but got caught up with the idea of being with a woman that was a child of God. He desired that type of relationship for himself and I was a refreshing break from Keira. Tommy loved me and I loved him but his guilt over that day confused him so we went into a territory we should have never been because we were only going to be friends. Julian loved me as I loved him unconditionally so when I lost him I spiraled back into my need to feel power again to keep from hurting. Malcolm was my crutch because when it came to sex I had full control and that was my temporary feeling of a false power which almost consumed me. Alonzo loved me, but he loved me in fear and I loved him but married him because I felt obligated and secure because of how we fell in love. The only other man I loved and knew loved me because of the turmoil we both suffered after our break up was...

My door flew open and all I heard were screams, "Mommy mommy," as the kids ran out onto the terrace and jumped into my lap. "Hey guys what are you doing back home so early?"
Mike walked in we are on an ice cream run and the kids wanted to see you because

they heard you were sick."

"Thanks you guys."

Mike looked around, "Where are the flowers JJ?"

"Oh mommy here," Julian Junior handed me a bouquet of crushed flowers. "They're beautiful, thank you." I said kissing them on the forehead. I looked up at Mike, "hey why don't you guys take theses flowers down stairs so we can put them in a vase and I'll meet you down there." After they ran out I grabbed Mike and asked, "Are you okay?"

"Yes why."

"Your eyes are telling me something different."

"It's Donna she's obsessed with the fact that she saw Julian at the hospital."

"Has she seen him again?"

"I'm not sure because I cut her off every time she brings it up." Mike sat down. "Alisha when I found out that Julian was a witness to that case I couldn't shake the fact that his death was a rouse. Hell Alisha we never saw his dead body because they cremated him before we got there so I want to believe Donna but I can't allow myself to."

"I know Mike I feel the same way." I wanted to tell him about the realistic dreams I've had about Julian and the fact that Ms.

Daniels saw and spoke to him but I didn't know if it was a dream or if I'm losing my mind from grief. "Alisha I'm sick over this and my health is failing because of it." I hugged Mike, "I'm here if you need me but you have five grandchildren depending on you." He smiled as we walked towards the stairs. They departed just as quick as they arrived.

Ms. Daniels and Mr. Avery walked in as I was putting the flowers on the table in the foyer. "Alisha was that Mike and the kids I saw pulling out of the subdivision?"
"Yes they came over to bring me some flowers after they heard I was sick."
"That was sweet."
"Where are you guys coming from?"
"We can't tell you." She said trying not to smile as she quickly ran downstairs. I walked into the kitchen to get something to snack on because I was feeling better and wanted to eat so I grabbed a bag of chips. Mr. Avery walked into the kitchen as I sat down. "I see you're feeling better here Jack sent this."
"Jack?"
"We went to his place for dinner and he asked about you and sent you your favorite meal when he found out you were sick."
"Great because I'm starving and I don't see

anything to eat that's not frozen. The kitchen is always dead when the kids are gone." I said frowning. He smiled and slowly walked out.

After I finished my meal I wanted something sweet as I was digging in the back of the refrigerator I was startled by Tommy walking up grabbing me. "What are you looking for in there?" he said. "Tommy you almost made me pee on myself, what are you doing?"
"I came to tell you the big news."
"Please don't tell me you slept with Naomi."
"No I told you I'm not going to have sex with a woman unless she's my wife."
"So what's the big news?"
"I asked her to marry me tonight."
"What?"
"Yes, I took everyone out but you because you were sick and this was a happy occasion."
"I understand, so is that why Ms. Daniels came in here smiling like that?"
"I guess so because she didn't seem too happy at the table when we announced it."
"Congratulations Tommy, I'm so happy for you." As we were hugging Ms. Daniels walked in with Naomi. "You can't do that anymore he's engaged now."
"Do what Mama?"

"They don't need to do intimate stuff like that because he has you for that."

"Mama she was just congratulating him on the engagement and they've been friends a long time so if they wanted to be together they could've a long time ago."

"Okay Naomi don't be stupid remember what happened with your husband and your father."

"Mama both of them were cheaters heck dad was cheating on his first wife when he met you and the whole time you were together but instead of seeing things as they really were you place the blame on something else. Mama he has two children younger than me and my husband was just like a mosquito always look for a warm wet place to land and then suck the life out of it. You can't compare a good man like Tommy to those sorry guys."

"Naomi I won't let you speak about your dead father like that he provided well for you." "Yes he did but he died on top of the lady down the street that was twenty years younger than him after she had his second child." Ms. Daniels stormed out of the room in tears saying, "I can't believe she's telling those lies on her father."

Naomi shook her head and said, I'm telling the truth she just refuses to face it. That's why we stop speaking to each other after she moved down here she was upset that I had a relationship with his outside children and my sister was moving down here so I let her stay with me. I'm just glad she met you Alisha because I met my future." She smiled and Tommy like a puppy ran over to her. "Come on Tommy let's take a walk before I go home."

After I closed the door behind the love birds Mr. Avery said, "So she calls him Tommy?"
"I forgot you were still up here."
"I just walked back in."
"She did call him Tommy didn't she."
"Yes she did." I smiled because I knew what she meant to him. She was really the one because he allowed her to call him Tommy. I knew then it was time for me to release my past hurts, hang ups, and the chains that kept me bound instead of just burying them deep inside of me and live life. I walked up the steps a little different and went to sleep peacefully without my Julian pillow, thoughts, or dreams.

Regrets of Obligation

I awake early that morning and worked out, something I hadn't done in a while. After my work out I drank my second blended meal without the protein this time. "Good morning Ms. Daniels how are you this morning?" she mumbled something incoherently about something not being right. Tommy walked in "Are you dressed yet Alisha?"

"No I am getting dressed now." I said running up stairs. Today was the big day for Mikael and Faith. Tommy was going with me because Naomi had a game to attend so Tommy would meet her there later. Tommy followed me upstairs, "This is why I hate riding with you"

"Tommy we have an hour before the ceremony starts."

"Are you sure?"

"Yes, so calm down."

"I'm just ready to see Naomi."

"I know." I yelled from the bathroom before I stepped into the shower. Tommy stepped out onto the terrace and called Naomi. Ms. Daniels burst into the room taking pictures. Tommy turned as he was talking and saw Ms. Daniels running around the bedroom. "I think you mother is having some issues because she just ran into the room taking pictures."

"Are you in Alisha's bedroom?"

"I'm on the terrace waiting for her to get dressed."

"Would it be possible for you to see her as she's getting dressed?"

"No I'm outside but even if I was in the room there's a separate entrance to the closet from the bathroom."

"My mom is obsessed with you and Alisha, was she like that before I started dating you?"

"No I guess she's trying to protect you."

"I know but I don't need her kind of protecting." They laughed and continued their conversation.

I walked into the bedroom after I got dressed. "Ms. Daniels, what are you doing?"

"I was looking for Thomas because I wanted to ask him something."

"Well I'm not sure where he is but you can call his phone since you have your phone in your hand."

"I'll ask Thomas later."

Tommy had walked back into the bedroom and said, "Ask me what?"

"Nothing it's not that important because I can't even remember."

"You mean you're ashamed because you ran in here snapping pictures trying to catch me and Alisha in the act."

"Ms. Daniels you should be ashamed of yourself." I gasped

"No I shouldn't he's engaged and you're a beautiful sexually aware woman that enjoys sexual pleasure a lot more than the average person so I'm trying to keep you honest."

"Ms. Daniels if I wanted to have sex I could but I choose not to until I get married because I've allowed that temporary satisfaction drive me into a sad reality."

"That's why I'm scared, you haven't been with a man since Alonzo died so you might lose control."

"Ms. Daniels I can understand your concerns but I'm not going to have sex with Tommy or any other man and lose my focus." She slowly turned to walk out not believing a word I said. Tommy and I departed so we could attend the wedding on time.

The wedding was being held at one of the oldest churches in the city so he had to pull some strings to get it. The reception was going to be held at the most expensive hotel downtown which was about ten miles from the church. I knew we were not going to the reception because Tommy wanted to make it to Jordan's first game, he was starting. Jasmine didn't go because she was going to an audition that day, so after I dropped Tommy off I was going to pick her up and take her to the game. Naomi and I bonded better than I thought considering the actions of Ms. Daniels. Tommy talked on the phone with Naomi until we parked at the church. We had gotten there with ten minutes to spare. "I hope this thing isn't long." Tommy said.

"It won't because they wanted simple but excellent."

"You mean quick but expensive, so he can make it up to her."

"Exactly," I said. We were escorted to our seats on the groom's side. After we sat down Tommy started pointing out the famous people at the wedding.

The church was traditionally decorated with flowers and a sheer attached on the aisle end of each pew. Mikael wore a white suit with green accents. Standing at the alter it appeared as if he had seen a ghost. Tommy leaned over, "He looks a little nervous."

"He'll be fine once he see his bride walking down the aisle towards him."

"I don't think so because he looks as if he's about to run."

"Stop Tommy," I laughed because he was right. He made two more comments and was cut off during the third as the music played.

They had six couples walk down the aisle and to my surprise Connie was Faith's Maid-of-honor as they slowly walked down the aisle Mikael started to sweat. Tommy gently elbowed me as he saw Mikael starting to sway. "He's going down." Tommy whispered. "I know but not yet," I whispered. As the ring bearer walked down the aisle Mikael began straightening up so Tommy whispered, "I guess he's getting..." Before he could finish we stood as the bride made her appearance. Faith was dressed in all white with pink and green accents representing life, purity, and the softness of love. Their colors and symbols throughout were described in the wedding program. The Pastor prayed before he performed the ceremony. Once he pronounced them man and wife he prayed again before releasing them to the world. Tommy was itching to leave but we had to wait until we were released. "Alisha, we leave out the side door because the game has already started."

"Wait two more minutes and we can walk out the front door."

"Alright," he said sitting down.

"Why are you sitting down lets go."

"I thought we were going to wait."

"I said two minutes."

"Oh I thought you said ten."

"Come on Tommy lets go."

"I'm right behind you." As we walked out I bumped into Connie, "What are you doing here?"

"I was invited by Faith and Mikael." Thinking if I said Faiths name first she would back off but not self-righteous know it all so I have to tell you about yourself Connie. "I'm sure she has no idea you're here and once you stop interfering in my brother's life by lowering yourself to be his side piece because you want to taste the life of the rich and famous which will not happen on my watch." Connie rotated her neck as she leaned towards me. I politely smiled but before I knew it laughed at her. "Connie you do know I'm wealthy, so unlike your brother whom I don't want I don't have to work to make money my money works for me to keep me in a life of luxury." She quickly turned up her nose and walked off mumbling, "But you still don't have a man." Tommy and I laughed as we walked out of the church and got in the car.

Tommy decided to drive and for the first five minutes of the drive there was an eerie quietness. As we sat at the light I could see Tommy staring at me as if he had seen a ghost. "Alisha, are you lonely?"
"No I'm not Tommy."
"Do you want a man?"
"The only man I desire is Julian but I'm okay being by myself."
"Did I let you down by falling for someone else?"
"Tommy we were meant to be friends not a couple, so no I'm happy because I think she's the one God had for you."
"Thanks Alisha." We continued to talk until we reached the park. Tommy parked and hurried in as I drove off to pick up Jasmine.

The same weekend of the wedding Mike and Mr. Avery made plans to play golf. Tommy wanted to go that morning but he knew he had to be at the wedding. While the men were on the golf course Donna and Ms. Daniels were at home with the kids doing crafts after breakfast. Millie was taking charge so she was bossing JJ and AJ around as usual. "Little Miss Millie, if

you don't give your brother back that glue you will be in your room for the next ten minutes." Ms. Daniels exclaimed standing at the other end of the table. "But JJ is doing it wrong the glue should be first." "Millie, give him the glue back or go to your room." Millie gave JJ the glue stick and walked towards AJ. "AJ let me help you since JJ can't follow instructions." "No, because you took my crayon." AJ pouted as he snatched away.
Donna walked over to Millie. "Come over here and paint my picture."
"Okay because boys can't follow instructions and mess everything up. Donna sat in a chair and posed for a portrait.

While Donna was getting her portrait done Ms. Daniels helped AJ paste objects on his picture. Suddenly Donna jumped up grabbing her stomach as she quickly ran into the bathroom. When she came out Ms. Daniels asked, "Is everything was alright?" "Yes Sarah but I feel so strange." As she uttered those words they heard sirens, "Oh my God," Donna screamed, "Its Mike!" She ran to the door as Ms. Daniels pulled out her phone to call Mr. Avery. Her first two calls went straight to voicemail but as she cleared the line to call him again her phone rung startling her, so she almost dropped it. "Honey is everything okay?" she blurted. "No, Mike just had a heart attack. Tell Ms. Pye to watch the kids while you take Donna to the hospital I'm going to get a ride with Sylvester," he was Mr. Avery's golf buddy Sylvester. "Don't tell Donna anything." Ms. Daniels called Ms. Pye. She walked the kids towards the house until she could see Ms. Pye standing on the porch. Ms. Daniels quickly turned and headed for the car and drove off. Donna was hysterical so Ms. Daniels silently prayed. "Sarah, I can't live without both of them."

"Yes you can because you have Julian Junior, Millie, AJ and Alisha." Donna leaned back and cried as she dwelled on Sarah's truth. When they pulled up to emergency Sylvester was standing on the curb. He helped Donna out of the car and rushed her into the waiting room. Ms. Daniels parked and rushed in but when she arrived Sylvester was the only person standing there. "Sarah, she's in the back saying her goodbyes."

"He's dead," She exclaimed in shock.

"He had a massive heart attack and died while he was on the tee. We were only playing the back nine today and we were in a cart so I don't understand."

"When God says its time its time, it doesn't

matter what you're doing." They continued their conversation while sitting in the waiting room.

As I was dropping Jasmine off my phone rang. I thought why is he calling, he's supposed to be on the golf course but then I looked at the time and realized I was late for our early dinner. Every other month we would get together so the men could play golf. The women would make crafts with the kids. We would all go out to eat at Jack restaurant and like clockwork Jerri would show up, so we came to expect his fake just popped up presence. I answered the phone, "Dad I'm on the way I had to drop off Jasmine."
"Good because Donna is going to need you."
"Why does she need me?"
"Mike just died."
"Wait, what happened to Mike?"
"He had a massive heart attack on the golf course."
"Where is he?"
"At General First"
"I'm on the way now." I called Tommy to let him know. Twenty minutes later I was in the waiting room and saw Mr. Avery talking to Ms. Daniels and Mr. Sylvester O'Bryan. I walked up, "Where is Donna?"
"They had to sedated her and admitted her

since they are keep her overnight for observation."

"Okay Dad." I said looking around in deep thought. "Have they put her in a room yet?"

"Yes she's in room 219." I walked off without saying a word.

I walked towards the elevator so I could check on Donna. When I got off the elevator I took a deep breath before I walked towards her room. When I walked in she was asleep. "Do you know the patient?"

"Yes she's my mother in-law."

"Really," the nurse said as she stood back and examined me looking surprised. "Yes really," I said walking closer to the bed as she walked out.

I knew it was hard for people to believe that we were family or that she would've allowed her son to marry me because the circles she would associate with wouldn't allow my tightly curled and sun kissed skin to marry into her family. Donna was disowned by some of her family members because she married a man that was beneath her. I always thought she was poor. I found out after Julian died that Donna was born with a silver spoon in her mouth but while in college she met Mike and the got married during her junior year because her father forbid her to date him, but she couldn't let him go. After her father found out she was still dating Mike her cut her off but she had a full scholarship to attend college so she finished college. After college they would experience the short lived joy of parenthood. Their first child Michael Lenard Carothers Junior passed less than six months after he was born.

At midnight I pulled out my phone to make a call and realized how late it was. I leaned back in the chair when I heard Donna mumbling something. "Donna is everything alright?"
"Alisha is that you?"
"Yes are you okay?"
"Yes but why am I here?"
I stood up and held her hand, "Donna, Mike had a massive heart attack and passed away earlier today." Tears flowed down her cheeks before she spoke. "He told me he wouldn't leave me but I knew he was sick." She sighed and fell back on the pillow. I rubbed her hand as she continued to silently to cry. After ten minutes she sat up, "Did you call Dawn?"
"Yes but my calls went directly to voice mail but I told her to call me a.s.a.p."
"Okay because Mike was her favorite Uncle and he loved her like a daughter."
"I know." I thought about how he funded

her business because he loved people that believed in working towards their dreams. He had a special fund setup to support people that he believed in.

Mike didn't want a funeral but a wake because he wanted to celebrate life. Mike's twin brother had Donna served at the wake, Rasheda's cousin had her served the next day, and his uncle served her two days after he passed. The wake was drama free and Donna was holding up well under the pressure. We knew Rasheda had her cousin handle the situation because she was in jail. Donna stayed with me for a month before she decided to return home.

Regrets of Family

After a few months we could finally settle Mike's will. Mike's family wanted everything and tried to prove he had never married Donna because it was not possible for a man like Mike to leave everything to a woman like her. When Mike was younger he was militant but he fell in love with this fair skinned soft spoken woman that reminded him of his mother. Mike's side of the family never accepted Donna because she was so light but so was his mother and she was treated the same way. They fought for less than six months because it was known that Mike had disowned his father's side of the family. Then they tried to use a son which was proved not to be his a month after he was born. The young man was the reason he ended up with Donna. His mother and Mike's father's side of the family never told him he was not Mike's son. Mike set up a trust fund for him with the agreement they would never contact him again. This and other family secrets came out and caused more issues for the family. They were the only ones fighting about the money but his mother's side wanted to control the company.

After the legal fight with his family Donna changed her will because she knew her family would try to take over because they wanted the money. Mike had given everything he had to Donna but started trust funds for all of his grandchildren which included all of my children, Rasheda's kids, and Dawn's son and stepdaughter. Mike always treated Dawn like she was his because her mother, his oldest sister, died in a boating accident when Dawn was ten so they took her in. She lived with them for two years because her father was in the military on active duty. At thirteen she went to live with her father and spent the summers with Mike and Donna.

Donna became ill again a few months after Mike's death. She had been staying with me on and off. As her health quickly begun to deteriorate she decided to go home. I tried to stop her, but she was ready to go home and relax since the mess was over. I called Dawn and asked her to stay with her. Donna came back after two days. Donna returned to the mansion after staying with me for another month. She had been home for less than twenty-four hours when the housekeeper found her in the bed dead. Consuela called me that morning, "Alisha, I just called 911 because I found Mrs. Carothers dead this morning." My heart sank and I pulled over to allow the news to sink in. "Thank you but I was on my way over anyway, so I'll be there in five minutes." When I turned into the estate my mind went wild with the memories from my first date with Julian to the day I drop Donna off yesterday. The closer I got to the main house tears flowed like an open facet. I called Dawn as I parked but it went to voice mail. "Hey Dawn I just called to tell..." I looked up to see her car in the distance so I got out and walked up to the house.

When I walked in Dawn met me with tears. "Hi Alisha, are you okay?"
"No I'm not but we will make it." We hugged as the doorbell rang. It was the coroner so I rushed into the bed room for one last glimpse of Donna. I kissed Donna one last time on the forehead, gave Dawn a hug, and turned to leave. "Alisha wait Donna gave me this for you last night." Dawn handed me an envelope. "What is this?"

"I don't know she just said that Julian wanted you to have it."

"But Julian's been gone for..." I paused and smiled at Dawn. I rushed to my car so I could see the contents of the envelope but tears clouded my view. I lay my head on the steering wheel and tried to focus.

After I regained my composure I called Ms. Daniels and informed her about Donna. I revealed to her that I was scared to tell Millie about Donna because she's experienced an abundance of death in her young life. I told her to allow Millie to go to school but I would pick her up. I wanted to tell all the kids at one time because Donna has been like a grandmother to all of them. I knew Millie would take it hard, since Donna's been at our house she and Millie were inseparable.

After seeing the contents of the envelope I was angry and amazed at the same time. I decided to drive to my office to figure out what I was going to do when my phone rang. "Hello"

"Hello Alisha, this is Rodney."

"Hi oh my I almost forgot we were meeting for brunch today."

"Yes and I'm calling because I want to meet at this new restaurant off highway 10 or is that late timing?"

"No, I was just talking to some girlfriends of mine about going there."

"Well will you try it with me?"

"Yes I will."

"Well lets meet at 11:30...I forgot the name."

"Undercover Dishes is the name." I laughed because I knew what the name meant.

"What's so funny?"

"The restaurant is owned by a post op transsexual and she opened it with her chef husband."

"Wait...never mind we will meet at 11:30."

"Okay."

"Is everything alright you seem different."

"Donna passed this morning and she gave me...I'll talk about it later." When we got off the phone I checked the time. I had at least three hours before I had to meet him.

When I walked into the house I could hear Olivia singing so I knew she was in the kitchen making herself coffee. "Olivia I'm not going to be here long," I yelled.

"Doc," she said as she ran into my office.

"What are you doing here so early?"

"I need to find a number and check out something."

"Is everything okay, should I be doing something?"

"I almost forgot to tell you Donna passed

this morning, so I'm not going to work today so I can tell the kids but I have to take care of some things first."

"Wait I just remembered you got this envelope this morning but it was just sitting on the steps."

"Really," I visually examined the package and put on a pair of latex gloves before I opened it. "Doc is that really necessary?"

"I know I'm doing the most as you say but being safe is better than regrets for not doing the most."

"Okay do you." When I opened the package I was in shock and quickly replaced them in the envelope throwing them in the trash.

"Olivia I have a brunch date at 11:30 so I'm going to work on something until ten please don't let me work past ten."

"Are you going out with that fine ass Pastor?" I glanced up at her trying not to smile. "He deserves more respect than that."

"Oh so you're saying he hasn't hit it yet?"

"Olivia really," I said shaking my head.

"Doc you're starting to act like those holy rollers now so be careful." I thought about what she said but I also remembered my vow to myself. I knew how much I wanted Rodney but I also knew how much I wanted to do things different this time. The packages I received today complicated things.

At ten minutes to ten I was in my car on my way to meet Rodney for lunch. My thoughts were invaded with Malcolm and Julian but I had to erase my past even if it was a reality in my present if I were moving forward with my life. I called Tommy so I could take my mind off the package and the men that changed my life forever. Before he said hello I screamed, "Tommy how is everything going?"

"No how are you handling the situation?"

"What situation?" I said fearfully.

"Donna...wait is something else going on?"

"No but I'm okay. I'm on my way to meet Rodney."

"You guys seem to be getting serious."

"No Tommy we are just friends."

"Did he say that or is that what you're trying to convince yourself you are?"

"He hasn't asked for more than that."

"So are you blind or just slow?"

"Tommy that's not nice," I smiled because I knew he was right.

"Alisha, this man has done everything right and given every sign that you're the one he wants to be with."

"Tommy I don't do actions alone because in our deepest desires we pick up on things that are not so."

"Alisha I know you're scared but…"

"Tommy I have something I think you should see before you say that."

"Alisha, Julian is gone and you can love again."

"I know but I'm so sexually attracted to Rodney I don't know if it's my lust or my true feelings."

"You and that little pocket between your legs need to come to an understanding."

"I am not going to have sex until I get married."

"But you are still having those graphic dreams about Julian?"

"Tommy I told…hold on this is Olivia."

"Hi Olivia what's up?"

"I just called because you got a bigger package and I think you need to come back to the office and sign for it."

"Well I can't so when I finish I'll come back to the office." I clicked over before she could respond. "Tommy, I'm here so I'll call you later.

When I walked in Rodney was there waiting. He had already ordered our drinks. "Hello beautiful." He said hugging me before he pulled out my chair. "Well hello, you seem different."

"I just made a big decision and today I will

walk into my destiny."

"Oh really, well I guess that's a blessing." I smiled and took a sip of my drink. "Alisha I forgot you just lost someone close to you."

"No that's not it."

"Then what's wrong?"

"Nothing I'm just in awe of you and your relationship with God."

"Thank you but like any relationship it takes time, patients, and work." I smiled as he squeezed my hand. "Alisha you're a good person and you've made poor choices but we all have. I wanted to wait but I think you need to know this now."

"What," I asked smiling.

"Alisha I've known you for years and even then I knew you were special but these past few months have allowed me to see you in a different way."

"What do you mean?"

"Alisha when we met you were ready to take over the world and instead of facing your pain you smothered it but now you face your issues or should I say, you face your hurt head on and you allow yourself to be rescued instead of lying to yourself causing more confusion in your life."

"Well you're right I've accepted the fact that God doesn't need me to help him but submit to Him and allow His will go forth."

"Alisha, you're a special woman and you're

going to make s very deserving man a wonderful wife."

"Thanks Rodney." I said thinking about Tommy being wrong, so when the waitress brought out our food the distraction cut my thoughts short. Rodney ordered the scrambled eggs with smoked sausage and I had the French toast casserole, we were already drinking mango smoothies.

We talked as we ate and I realized that Rodney was ready to settle down with the Godly woman he fell in love with. I knew Tommy was wrong but I wished it was as he said because I really liked Rodney. I knew I had ruined my life and a man of God couldn't be with a woman like me because his congregation wouldn't accept me. "Hey beautiful, what's on our mind," he asked. "Nothing."

"Well from here it seems like a lot." He laughed and I joined in after taking a sip of my smoothie. "Come on Alisha."

"Well I've lost so many love ones in less than five years. I feel like I'm destined to be alone."

"I don't know how to answer that but I don't think you will be alone forever because God is always with you and you have so much love to give."

"Thanks Rodney I needed that."

"You deserve it." He said as he waived for the waitress. "So when are you going to settle down?"

"When God says we are ready but not until then."

"Really so do you know who she is?"

"Yes because she already has my heart." Before I could respond the waitress was at the table with the check. "Well I have to pick up the kids and tell them about Donna so I needed this time with you."

"Alisha, I've always loved being a friend to you but this go around is better than the first because we've been able to respect our vow to abstain."

"You're right." I said. We continued to talk as we walked to my car. He opened my door and gave me a hug before I got in.

When I arrived at the school to pick up Millie and Julian I thought about the package that contained the pictures. I glanced at them once again before pushing them under the driver's seat. I walked into the office and Julian ran to me. "Mommy I missed you and Momzie this morning."

"Well I wanted to talk to you guys about Momzie." I told him to get his book bag while I signed them out of school. Julian asked a million questions as we walked to the car and they continued until we got home. Julian jumped out of the car and ran in the house. Millie had not said anything until I opened the car door. "Mommy what happened to Momzie?"

"What?" I was so shocked by her question that I couldn't answer her. "Mommy is Momzie dead?"

"Yes Millie he passed last night."

"Mommy, why is everyone we love dying?"

"Baby that's life and people die every day but we must continue to live on."

"I knew Momzie was going to die but DJ, My daddy, and Papa Mike was not sick like her they were not supposed to die." I put my arms around Millie as she cried for about ten minutes. "What are we going to do for JJ because she was his grandmother?"

"I'm not sure Millie." I said as we walked into the house.

I walked into the family room holding Millie's hand. "Hi Ms. Daniels where is Julian?"

"He ran into the bathroom a minute ago." She said looking towards the bathroom. A few minutes later he came running out and sat on the floor next to his brother and continued to watch TV. "Will you guys turn off the TV for a minute because I need to talk to you about something?"

"Mommy I don't want to know because Super Good is about to defeat the Evil Minis." Julian quickly said.

"Turn off that TV right now," Millie screamed as she picked up the remote. "Go ahead Mommy." She sat in the big chair and called AJ to come over and sit in her lap. I took a deep breath and said, "Momzie has passed away."
"What do you mean?" Julian asked as tears formed in his eyes.
"Momzie is with your Daddy and Papa Mike now so she's in good hands."
"Mommy you mean she's with God."
"Yes Millie."
"But why Mommy what did she do wrong?"
"Julian you don't have to do anything wrong but when God says it's time to go it's time to go."
"That's not fair God is taking everybody from me." Julian screamed and ran into my arms. Millie jumped up and ran over with tears as AJ sat in the chair looking lost. I held the two of them a tight as I could and tried to fight back the tears forming in my eyes. Ms. Daniels picked up AJ when his lip begun to quiver and tear rolled down her cheeks. "Who wants to go get some ice cream with the winner?" Tommy yelled as he walked into the room. "What's

going…Alisha I forgot, please forgive me."
"That's alright Tommy." I smiled and
squeeze the children a little tighter. Ms.
Daniels placed AJ in my arms and departed
with Tommy. We sat there until the
children fell asleep.

When Ms. Daniels and Mr. Avery got back
they took the children upstairs to their bed.
After they removed AJ I awake, "Hey how
was dinner?"
"It was okay and Thomas sent you a plate."
Ms. Daniels whispered as she picked up AJ.
"He said he sent it because you're greedy,"
Mr. Avery bellowed as he walked out of the
room carrying JJ. I laughed as I carried a
heavy Millie to bed.

The house was extra quite for the next
couple of days after the funeral. The
children came out of their shell completely
after a week. Their appetites returned as
well. I was back to my normal schedule and
after the reading of the will the fight was
over. Dawn inherited the estate and I
received more stocks and some money. The
kids received another trust fund. Donna's
family couldn't fight because she put
stipulations in her will. Her family hated
the fact that she married such a dark
skinned poor man and that his family

couldn't pass the paper bag test but they
loved his mom.

Regrets of Leaving

Tommy and I were sitting on the front porch talking about life when we saw a cab pull up to his house. "Tommy who's that and why didn't you tell me you were having company?"

"I don't know but I think they are at the wrong house. Let me stop them before they wake up my family." Tommy ran home but I stood on the porch to be nosey. When the woman got out of the car I knew who it was so I ran towards his house. When I got there I could see the fear and confusion in Tommy's eyes. "Isabella what are you doing here?" I asked. "Alisha this is my house, my husband, and my kids so you can go back to your house."

"What in the hell are you doing here?" Tommy said.

"Thomas I came back home didn't you miss me?"

"No he didn't, so get back in the cab and disappear like you did over two years ago."

"Alisha I'm trying to be nice but if you don't take your lonely...wait are you and Thomas?"

"Isabella you need to leave because I've moved on." Tommy said.

"I'm not going anywhere because I'm here to get my family back." She paid the driver and he drove off quickly. "Alisha you had your chance but I gave Thomas his family and he got over you because of me."

"No you didn't because Alisha has always come before your selfish, self-centered lying behind," Tommy raised his hands as he walked off. "Thomas what's wrong with you?"

"You need to leave because..."

"What is going on out here?" Naomi said as Tommy walked onto the porch. "Nothing babe so go back to bed."

"No because I could hear you when I came down stairs to get a glass of water."

"Who is this woman and why is she calling you Tommy?"

"This is my wife Naomi and we want you to leave."

"But I'm your wife and where are my kids?"

"You abandoned them remember now leave or I'll call the police."

"So what he got tired of screwing a hoe so he married a housewife?" Isabella barked looking at me.

"Well it takes one to know that since you aborted all those babies because you had no idea which ones belonged to Tommy."

"You bitch," Isabella screamed as she tried to slap me.

"Isabella, leave now." Tommy whispered through clenched teeth.

"But I don't have anywhere to go. We're still married and I wanted to see the kids."

"I'll take her to a hotel and give her some money."

"Alisha this s between me and my husband you are the reason we broke up in the first place. You never change do you?"

"You are why you left so I divorced you and got remarried."

"You can't divorce me without my consent."

"You signed the papers remember."

"I was upset and wanted to prove a point to you so that doesn't count."

"In a court of law it does." Tommy turned and walked into the house closing and locking the door behind him. Isabella ran to the door but before she could knock I said, "You touch that door and I'll snatch you bald." I walked closer to her. "Now you can get a room and we settle this like adults tomorrow or we can call 911, your choice." Isabella conceded so I took her to a hotel and dropped her off.

Tommy called me early the next morning, "Alisha everything's crazy."

"What's wrong?

"Naomi thinks I cheated on Isabella with you and that Millie is my daughter."
"Why in the world would...never mind it was her mother."
"Why would Ms. Daniels tell her those lies?"
"She didn't want Naomi to date you."
"What?"
"Tommy that's the past so where is Naomi now?"
"She went to work but she asked for a divorce before she walked out."
"Tommy everything is going to be alright."
"I wish Isabella would've stayed where she was."
"I know so are you going to talk to her and see what she wants?"
"I know what she wants and it's not me or the kids it's the money."
"Why would you think that?"
"Because a few weeks ago I got a call from her mother she left a message on my answering machine asking for 10,000 dollars so he could get Isabella medical care. I never returned the call."
"Isabella misses the kids because they tell me she calls all the time."
"That's not true. Before I started dating Naomi I would tell the kids that so they would sleep at night."
"What are you going to do Tommy?"
"Nothing unless she tries to see the kids

then I'll pay her off but she would have to sign documentation first." Tommy's phone clicked. "Hold on Alisha." He clicked over "Hello," He clicked back over, "Alisha this is her so I'm going to merge the calls but mute your phone okay." He merged the calls. "I'm back Isabella, so what do you want?"

"I want to see the kids because they deserve to be with me."

"You should've thought about that before you abandoned them."

"Thomas you know you were beating me so I had to escape."

"Why didn't you take them if I was beating you liar?"

"I didn't have any money so I couldn't take them with me."

"Really now your bank account had over 40,000 dollars when you left but there was over 80,000 the week before you left and you took out over 100,000 from our joint account the day you disappeared."

"I didn't know I had that money and your trick Alisha must have taken it because I didn't."

"It's funny that the money was withdrawn by a woman that looked like you and the remaining money was transferred to a different account."

"You are lying because I was in a shelter and I called Alisha every day to check on the kids."

"Isabella you keep living in that fantasy and tell me what you really want."

"I need my money so I can get a place for me and the kids."

"Isabella you haven't called or reached out to our kids since you left so why now?"

"I need money Thomas because I'm sick and want to reconnect with the kids."

"When do you want to see the kids and how much money do you want?"

"100,000 dollars in about an hour and you can bring it to the hotel because Alisha knows where I'm staying."

"The kids are in school so it will be tonight."

"You can give me the money and then I can see the kids later."

"No we can do it at the same time or not at all."

"Thomas I can get a court to get the kids and then you would have to pay me child support and I'll move back home so you won't be able to see them again."

"I have custody so you're the one that's behind on your payments."

"You are so evil and you're supposed to be a Godly man, well that's a lie."

"Isabella if I give you the money you must signed documentation to the fact."

"No I will not but I will see you in court."

"Go for it baby." Tommy hung up on both of

us so I called him back. "What," he yelled.

"Tommy you hung up on me."

"I'm sorry Alisha but that woman..." he growled.

"Calm down Tommy she's not going to court with this."

"I know but I don't want to give her a dime and we were trying to adopt each other's children."

"You are, man that's great?"

"It was going to be a surprise."

"So what are you going to do now?"

"Talk to Ms. Daniels first and then patch things up with my wife."

"I'll be praying for you Tommy. Talk to you later." We hung up and I got dressed for work.

When I got to work Olivia was on the porch watering the plants. "Good morning Olivia."

"Morning Doc." As I walked up the steps she said, "You have someone in your office." I look a little puzzled. "Who," I whispered. "Naomi, she's been here for over an hour." "Is she in my office or the living room?" "Living room," Olivia whispered. I walked in but she was not in the living room so I walked to my office and unlocked the door. "Alisha you're finally here." She said walking up behind me.

"Yes would you like to talk?"

"I just need you to answer some questions."

"Ask away but if I feel like it's none of your business I'll tell you so."

"Are you having sex with Tommy?"

"No."

"Did you have sex with Tommy while he was with Isabella?"

"No."

"Do you want Tommy for yourself?"

"No."

"Is Tommy Millie's biological father?"

"No."

"Have you had sex with Tommy since my mother has worked for you?"

"No."

"Have you had any sexual contact with Tommy since my mother has been working with you?"

"No."

"Alisha why is Isabella back and did you cause their marriage to crumble?"

"I don't know and no."

"Alisha my mom told me some things about you and Tommy so after hearing Isabella last night I wonder if they're true."

"No they're not but I can tell you Isabella cheated on Tommy, had several abortions, and ran off with her first boyfriend and returned to her homeland because that's what she wanted to do."

"What about your relationship with him?"

"What about it?"

"Men and women can't have what you have and not be sexually attracted to each other."

"Why because that's the lie the world tells us?" I knew the truth would hurt her.

"Alisha I envy the relationship you have with my husband."

"If I were a man would you envy our relationship?"

"No, but that's different."

"Why because of your own insecurities?"

"That's not fair Alisha because when Tommy wants to make a major decision he comes to you first."

"That's where you're wrong; he runs to my backyard and sits on the swing by himself. Tommy has been doing that for years because it reminds him of his talks with Ma Carrie."

"So he's been alone in your backyard all this time?"

"Yes," I said smiling as she started laughing.

"Forgive me Alisha that was silly."

"No it wasn't but you need to call your husband and let him know how you really feel before he talks to your mother."

"Why would he talk to my mother?"

"Because she's the one that told you all of that crap so I told him where it came from and he wants to talk to her about it."

"Oh my god where's my phone, thanks Alisha bye." She ran out and Olivia ran in, "so what going on in the never ending drama of Alisha always caught in the middle because she's the go to person?"

"Isabella is back and told Naomi I was having sex with Tommy."

"Why is she back?" Olivia frowned.

"I'm not sure but I think it's for money."

"Well speaking of money where's that envelope I gave you a few months ago?"

"What envelope?"

"The one you stuck in your file cabinet." She said rocking back and forth as she nodded towards my file cabinet. I thought I threw them away.

"That was nothing just some pictures of Alonzo on the beach with Malcolm that Lealtà photo shopped because she's trying to upset me."

"Can't you call the police on her for that because she came to your house."

"Olivia she has issues so I'm not going to let it bother me."

"Do you have the pictures?"

"Yes and here get rid of them."

"I think you should have her investigated."

"Leave it alone please."
"But how do you know they are fake?"
"Think about it would Alonzo be with Malcolm?"

"You're right." Olivia took the pictures into the kitchen and shredded them.

A few hours later as I was working on the books so I could send them off to my CPA when my private line rang. I was a little shocked so I quickly answered it, "Hello"
"Hi Alisha its Deuces."
"Hey Deuce is everything alright?"
"No they rushed dad to the hospital a few hours ago and mom wanted me to call you so you could come down here."
"Okay I'm on the way." I finished up the report and hit send before I snatched up my belongings. "Olivia I'm on my way to the hospital to see Charles."
"What happened?"
"I'm not sure but he son just called me."
"Be careful and call me."
"Okay," I said as I ran out the door.

As I drove to the hospital I thought about Tommy and his issue with Isabella but I knew I had to stay out of it to respect Naomi. My thoughts flowed to Rodney but they rested on the kids and the turmoil they suffered over the past few years. I decided to give them a monthly treat and I thought a vacation would be better and give them great memories. I started planning the perfect vacation in my head. By the time I arrived at the hospital I planned three trips. I wrote them down before I got out of the car so I could decide which trip we would take first.

When I got to the Hospital I checked my phone. Deuces had text me a room number because Charles had been admitted. When I got on the elevator a sudden chill came over me as I thought about my last few visits to a hospital and the outcome was not pleasing. I took a deep breath before entering the room. "Hello Richmond family." Mark and Deuces looked up and smiled. "Hello Alisha," Gladys's said as she walked over to me, "Thank you for coming." "Anytime but where is he?" "They took him for test so Andrea went with him and Elaine had to pick up the kids." "Well how is he?" "Dad's a solider so he's good they wanted to run a few more test and keep him overnight for observation." It was good to hear some good news for a change. "Why did you want me to come?" "Dad wanted you to here Alisha so you could sign this paperwork before he changed his mind."

"What is this?"

"He wants you to take over his businesses until Elaine is ready to take over."

"When will she be ready to take over?"

"That's where you come in and how long it takes for you to train her." Charles said as the wheeled him into the room. "Train her to do what?" I asked.

"How to manage her time as a mother, wife, and business woman," Charles said as they eased him into the bed.

"I can't teach that because she has to have that within her already."

"She's my daughter so it has to be there."

"Has she changed in the last year because the Elaine I know is lazy, selfish, and rude."

"Okay she's a little rough around the edges but you can do the impossible Alisha." Deuces said as he grabbed my hand smiling.

"Deuces, why are you smiling so hard at your daddy's rejected leftovers?" Andrea said sarcastically.

"Does your brain ever connect with you hatful mouth?"

"Whatever," she said as she stormed out of the room. Charles sat up in the bed and looked at his son, "That's a good question Deuce."

"Dad, come on really." Mark laughed because he knew how his brother felt about me. "What's so funny Mark is there something you need to tell me?"

"No dad I don't have anything to say." Gladys chimed in, "Alisha will you help her?"

"I don't know because I know her and she's a good person but she's mean if things don't go her way." I said shaking my head, I scratched my forehead. Deuces turned to me, "Give it a week and if she works out we can work out a deal."

"Let me pray about it first."

"Thanks Alisha." Charles said smiling.

"Is there anything else I can do?"

"No we're good," Deuces said. When I turned to leave Andrea bumped into me. "I'm not into women Andrea so you can keep that crap to yourself." Everyone started laughing as she stomped over to her father pouting.

When I left the hospital I returned the two missed calls from Tommy and the text from Rodney. Rodney text me asking how I was doing so I replied and let him know I would talk to him later. I called Tommy without listening to his messages. "Alisha what took you so long to call me back?" Before I could respond he started ranting.

"Isabella has a lawyer and a court date for custody of the kids so I don't know what to do."

"First calm down and second have you talked to your wife."

"Yes and she told me to call you."

"Okay take a deep breath and call your father in law."

"Why would I call her father?"

"No Natasha's father Phil or Paul or something."

"You're right I almost forgot about him." Tommy hung up the phone immediately. I drove back to my office thinking about what Olivia said.

I walked into my office with a mission so I didn't see the person sitting on the sofa as I unlocked the door, quickly closing the door behind me. I sat at my desk and pulled out the vacation list and started searching when Olivia knocked on the door. "Alisha you have a client waiting on you."

"Who, I don't have any appointments?"

"He said he's here on behalf of Malcolm Maldad's estate."

"I didn't get...okay tell him I'll be with him in a moment."

"Yes ma'am." Olivia walked out. After she walked out I pulled out a picture of Malcolm that I saved for Millie. I wrote on a

sticky pad and stuck it to my computer screen before I walked out. Hello Mr..."
"Scott, Lloyd Scott but you can call me Lloyd." We shook hands and sat down. "Like I told your Assistant I'm here to talk about Mr. Malcolm Diablo Maldad's estate."

"But he has a family so why would you be talking to me instead of his wife?"
"We had trouble locating you at the address we were given so we came out to locate you in person to fulfill his wishes."
"What wishes?"
He pulled out an envelope from his briefcase. "Milagro Vida Maldad is his daughter, right?"
"Her last name is Coleman-Avery but yes she is his biological daughter."
"Well he left his daughter this package." He handed me the envelope. "He opened several accounts and she's the beneficiary so they were closed after his death so here's a check for the accounts per his instructions."
"Lloyd is this legal because he has a wife and children?"
"Yes because of his will and it was not disputed." He handed me the check and gave me paperwork to sign showing I received the check and other documents. "Thank you Ms. Coleman." We shook hands

and I walked him to the door. I was a little confused but I shook it off and went back to planning.

I walked into my office and started writing after looking at the sticky note. As I wrote a plan I realized the reason I made poor choices in my life. I kept taking my eyes off Jesus. I couldn't do the supernatural if I was assisting the One that needed no assistance. I was always that go too person so no one prayed because I became their savior but I was a hindrance because they had faith in flesh instead of spirit. I got the revelation to help Elaine for a month and then retire completely. Resign from the board over the Community Center within two years. The last thing I would do is sell my house and become a full time mom. I prayed and read a few scriptures before I started my search on vacation spots.

I was searching when Olivia came in with some flowers. "Doc these were just delivered and there's a card, so who are they from?" "Olivia I have no idea." I read the card but there was not a name. "They didn't put a name on the card."
"What does the card say."
"Don't ever forget about me because I will always love what we share."

"Maybe it's the Pastor."

"No he wouldn't do that."

"Could they be from Malcolm," she asked looking uncertain.

"He is dead." I said looking up at her sideways. "Are you sure because weird things are happening like the envelope, the letters, and that lawyer."

"What letters?"

"Oh well they came last weekend."

"Olivia where are they?"

"In your office mail that I left on the table while you were talking to the lawyer," she said as she ran out the door. "Here's your mail and the letters are on top."

"Thanks," I said as I opened the letter. Olivia was waiting impatiently as I opened the letter. "What does it say?" She grabbed the envelope and inspected it before I could respond. "Is it from him?"

"Olivia, can I read it first!"

"Well you're taking too long so let me open the other one."

"No so sit down until I finish or go to your desk."

"Okay," she said pouting. I continued to read the letter and realized it was from Lealtà so I shredded it. "What are you doing?"

"It was from Lealtà."

"What did she say?"

"She blames me for his death."

"You didn't shoot him."

"I know it's her grief." I read the second letter but that letter was from him before he died but was sent from his lawyers in Jamaica. "What does it say?"

"Nothing," I said looking around frantically, "Nothing."

"Let me know when you want to talk." She eased out of my office.

I went home an hour later and found out that Tommy had an appointment with his lawyer in two days and the case looked good in his favor. Isabella was trying to convince Tommy to give her money so she would drop the case. His lawyer told him to record all of his calls with her but let her know she was being recorded. When it was time to go to court Isabella didn't show up but her lawyer did with an excuse. The judge wanted to postpone the case until the lawyer could contact her but Tommy's lawyer was trying to have the case dismissed. Two hours later Isabella appeared and decided to fight for the kids. I had given her 100,000 to drop the case but she wanted money from Tommy too. After the judge heard the tape recordings of Isabella asking for money in exchange for the kids the judge gave her supervised visitation. She also chastised her for being so selfish to the kids because she wouldn't see them unless Tommy gave her money but showed up at the school and surprised them causing confusion. Isabella went back home empty handed and angry. When she showed up for court I put a stop payment on the check. She didn't even have enough sense to cash the check first.

After putting the kids to bed I went to bed thinking about the letter Malcolm wrote before he died. I couldn't believe he wanted to be with me and raise Millie and raise the boys as if they were his own. I knew Malcolm was controlling and abusive but there was a part of him that I desired before I met the real him. I was upset because he took Julian away from me but gave me a beautiful daughter. I knew one day I would have to tell her who he was so I had to hold onto the goodness of who he was for Millie's sake.

Regrets of Moving On

After I trained Elaine I sold my portion of the business to Charles and he allowed Deuces to take over. Years ago Deuces and I talked until he found out I didn't put out and he stop talking to me. I thought it was strange because I dated his father , so I could never date or get serious with him. Elaine refused to let go of her rudeness so they lost a few business deals. Charles fired her and hired one of Gladys's nieces. After I retired from my job with Charles the kids and I went on our first weekend vacation and it was just the four of us.

The second trip was going to be for a week and Ms. Daniels was having some issues with me going on a vacation with just my kids. "Alisha, are you sure you don't want me to come?"
"Ms. Daniels I've never been on a vacation and it was just me and my children."
"I know so why are you doing it now I'm sure Tommy and his family want to get away."
"Ms. Daniels we are going to the Pocono's

on Friday and it will only be the four of us."
"Alisha have I done something to upset you because I always go on the family vacations with you."
"No, but you have a husband and a daughter and grandchildren that you need to focus on. I need to focus on and give my children special memories with me."
"Alisha you're a young woman so you will have plenty of..."
"Look at Julian and Alonzo they were young so I'm not counting on a tomorrow but living life day by day as if it were my last"
"Alisha you need us."
"Ms. Daniels that's the problem I've needed you too much and it has caused me to become focused on my work when things happen instead of the kids because I knew you will take care of them."
"Alisha I refuse to let you take my babies from me."
"I'm not taking them away but I am giving them more of me."
"That's just not right," she said in a huff as she walked away.

We were leaving out Friday after the kids got out of school. The week before our trip I planned a spa day for Millie and myself on Tuesday. The boys wanted to eat at Dogs Dogs, which was a smorgasbord of hotdogs from around the world, so we went there Wednesday for dinner. I told them our itinerary for the trip. They were excited but wanted Mama D, Papa Avery, and Tommy's family to come. After I explained why we were going alone they understood. On the ride home the boys fell asleep. Millie screamed, "Mommy, are you going to die." She yelled so loud that I was startled. I regained myself, "Millie we are all going to die someday but I don't know when or how."

"No Mommy I mean now," she said as tears flowed down her cheeks. I tried to stay calm because Julian woke up after he heard her yell. "No Millie, I'm doing this because I've missed so much with my family because I work all the time and I promised DJ before he died that I would slow down."

"My daddy didn't want you to work Mommy?"

"No he didn't and I was about to retire when he passed."

"Why did my Daddy ask you to stop working?"

"Because he wanted to travel more so I decided to live out his dream." I didn't tell them about the children he wanted but it caused me to wonder. I don't know if the kids sensed my pain or if they were distracted but the car ride was quiet until we got home.

When I walked in the door Mr. Avery was standing in the foyer with is arms folded. "Mille take you brothers upstairs so you guys can take a bath and get ready for bed, I'll be up in a moment." After the kids were out of sight I tuned towards Mr. Avery, "Dad is something wrong?"
"Yes, it's my wife?"
"What's wrong with Ms. Daniels?"
"You tell me she said you hurt her."
"Dad I told her I wanted to spend some quality time with my children."
"That's not what she said."
"What did she say?"
"You wanted to take the kids away from her because she's closer to them than you are."
"What, okay I never said that but I'm not going to change my plans because I've sacrificed every family trip to include her, then her grandchildren, and now Tommy and his family. This is a trip for me and my children Dad because I've given everyone what they needed except me." As tears flowed Mr. Avery embrace me, "Alisha I understand and you've gone through a lot. There's something I want to talk to you about." We walked into the living room and sat down. "Alisha I finally sold Alonzo's

house so with the money from both houses and the children being older I believe it's time for us to move on and live out our life without taking care of our grandchildren and become visiting grandparents."

"I know Dad that's why I hired a Ms. Pye but Ms. Daniels feels as if she has to continue to work."
"Alisha I haven't told her yet but we will be moving out within the next month or two."
"We'll when are you going to tell her?"
"I guess while you're on vacation with the kids."
"Are you sure because I don't want you to leave on bad terms or because you think I don't want you here."
"Alisha you could never be on my bad side and she'll get over it." He laughed.
"Okay, I'll let you handle that." As I stood to leave Ms. Daniels walked in. "What are y'all sitting in the dark talking about?"
"Ms. Daniels I was on my way upstairs to get the kids ready for bed so goodnight."
"Alisha I'll be up there in a minute to help you."
"Honey let her do it so you can come downstairs and help me." He said grabbing her around the waist. "We have plenty of time for that but I need to check on the babies first."

"Sarah let her take care of her kids so you can do your wifely duties."

"Is that what you were talking about, I knew she wanted me out of the way but I never thought she would use you to do it."

"Sarah I've been complaining about the time you spend taking care of the children since Alisha hired Sophia (Ms. Pye)."

"Your wife was right Alisha has you wrapped around her finger or has she screwed you too?" She said as she stormed out of the room. Mr. Avery got up and walked out the front door.

The next morning during breakfast it was chilly and Mr. Avery was missing. "Good morning Ms. Daniels."

"Alisha," she said without looking at me.

"Good morning Mommy the kids screamed."

"Good morning babies," I said as I kissed each of them on the forehead. "Where's your Pops?"

"He's on the golf course with Tommy so you have to take us to school." Millie said looking at Ms. Daniels. "Well are you finished with your breakfast so we can go?"

"Mama D I thought you said Mommy wouldn't have time for us?" Julian blurted out. I looked at her and rolled my eyes but never responded. I walked upstairs to call Tommy and remembered I needed to leave him out of it. When I returned to the kitchen the kids were ready and waiting on me.

   After I dropped the kids off my phone rang, "Hello."
"Alisha, forgive me I but I over slept."
"Where are you?"
"I went to a hotel last night. Alisha if we don't move out I think I'll leave her."
"Dad, come on you fought harder for your first wife."
"That's just it I'm too old to do this again."
"I understand, so go talk to her."
"I'm on my way home now."
"She told the kids you were with Tommy playing golf."
"Thanks but she knew I was gone because she called me we argued and I hung up so she called back and I didn't answer."
"Dad you have to make up because I will feel responsible."
"This is not your fault it was because of you I found my beautiful wife."
"Okay Dad. Hold on, Tommy is on the other line so I'll talk to you later." I quickly clicked over. "Hey Tommy what's up?"
"Naomi is pregnant and were moving back home."
"Wait what?"
"I know but my father said they need an

Elder so I'm selling the house and we're moving home at the end of the month."
"We'll have you talked to Ms. Daniels?"
"No because we just made the decision yesterday and I was supposed to keep it secret but I can't keep anything from you."
"When did you find out about the baby?"
"Monday but we want to see a doctor to be sure and her appointment is Friday."

"So you think Ms. Daniels is going to handle that well?"
"She's so mad at you right now for taking your kids away that I don't believe it would matter."
"I just wanted to have..."
"You don't have to explain Naomi and I have already talked about it so we understand and are glad because she's let up on her some by giving her the freedom to raise her own kids."
"Dang my phone is hot today this is Rodney calling so..."
"Bye go talk to your husband."
"We are not dating." I said as I was clicking over. "Hi Rodney, how are you."
"Great Alisha, how have you been?"
"I'm great so how was the mission trip?"
"It was awesome but I would like to see you today because I want to talk to you about something."

"When and what time would you like to meet Rodney?"
"Can I meet you at your office around ten?"
"Yes I'm on my way there now."
"Okay I'll see you in an hour."

I drove to my office thinking about Rodney's news. I knew he was going to tell me that he got married because the woman he had been dating was pressuring him for a commitment. She would be the perfect first lady because the elders picked her out for him and the congregation loved her. I attended his church twice and my first visit was nice but the second one was a little different. The ladies rolled their eyes or turned up their noses but a few of the deacons flirted with me. I was attracted to Rodney and my lustful feelings no longer existed. After I worked on my sexual desire by being honest with myself and why I felt I needed to have sex, I was released from the bondage that held me for years. I spent quite time with God, prayed, and read scripture but it was being brutally honest with myself that caused me to change my focus and see my self-worth the way God saw me. I rededicated my life and spent more time focusing on my children than the needs of others. The biggest help was

Rodney he helped walk me through my issues like he did to overcome his.

I sat in my car for about twenty minutes and pondered my life with Julian. As I was getting out of the car I dropped my phone between the side of my seat so I reached under the seat and grabbed the envelope I had put under there when Donna passed. Before I could open it there was a knock on my passenger side window that startled me. Rodney was waving at me. I had been in the car a lot longer than I thought. I got out of the car, "Hi Rodney you're early." I said getting out of the car. "Only five minutes." He said coming around to give me a hug as I stuck the envelope in my bag. "Come on lets go in the house so you can tell me the big news."

"Big news did someone call you?"

"No I just figured it out."

"Really so..."

"It's about time you decided..." Olivia shouted. "This package was on the door step Monday evening and since I couldn't call you I have been going crazy waiting on you to get here."

"Well you have to wait a little longer." I smiled as I walked to my door. "Alisha, don't do this, oh hi Rodney."

"Hello Olivia." Rodney laughed, "Don't

worry I won't be long."

"Well first of all congratulations."

"Well it was a mission trip but I guess having the ability to go over there and make it back safe and sound is a feat."

"No I'm talking about you getting married."

"When did I get married Alisha?"

"Isn't that your big news?"

"I said I wanted to talk to you about something." I was embarrassed because I let my mind wonder into la la land. "Forgive me, so what did you want talk about?"

"I want you to help our Church start a counseling center."

"Okay, so what do you need from me?"

"It's all in this business plan so pray, read it over, and pray again so God can lead you."

"Okay I'll call you next week."

We stood up and shook hands. "Have a good day." I walked Rodney to the door.

Before I could close the door Olivia was behind me with the package. "Okay now that he is gone can we open it?"

"Yes but I'm sure they're just picture from Lealtà to upset me."

"Well I'll be the judge of that." I opened the package and just as I thought more pictures of Malcolm on the beach. "I told you but you can have them if you want."

"Alisha do you ever miss him?"

"Miss who?" I knew who she was talking about and I was over him but didn't realize it until she asked me that she still loved him. "Malcolm!" She said full of excitement "No I don't."

"Well I do and I wish he was still alive so we could spend the rest of our lives together."

"Olivia did you forget the fact that he beat you so bad you lost your child?"

"He was upset because you hurt him."

"Olivia, do you hear the words coming out of your mouth or are you just talking without thinking?"

"Yes and I also know you wouldn't stop me from dating him because I'm still in love with him."

"Olivia, shred the pictures and print out the letters from yesterday so I can proof them before you send them out." I said walking away.

"Alisha I contacted Lealtà so I could talk to her bout Malcolm."

"Why in the Hell would you do that?"

"I miss him. Alisha I was going to be the mother of his child."

"I understand." I walked back into my office and pondered what Olivia said. It was almost unbelievable but then I thought about how caring, gentle and loving he could be. I wanted to be alone if he was what I had to be with but she really missed him. I thought about how I would tell Millie about him and my heart sank.

I stopped to get pizza on my way home because we were having a pizza night before we went on the trip. Everybody came over to eat pizza. After we blessed the food the doorbell rang. "Who in the world could that be?" Ms. Daniels said looking around the table to make sure everyone was there. "I'll get it you guys continue to eat." I ran to the door and to my surprise it was Rodney. "Is everything alright?"
Yes Alisha, I came over to enjoy the pizza."
"Who invited you?" I said smiling.
"His new golf buddy," Tommy said as he walked in. "Good evening Thomas thanks for the invite."
"Rodney you can go into the dining room with everyone else." I said as we walked towards the dining room I snatched Tommy back. "Why did you invite him?"
"Because when everyone moves on and out you are going to need someone to protect you."
"Tommy I moved up here and lived by myself for years remember."
"Alisha that was different you were young and free."

"I had Millie?"

"You've suffered a lot and I want you to have a support system."

"Tommy you're trying to play match maker and you know he's engaged."

"Alisha..."

"What is he doing here?" Ms. Daniels asked angrily cutting Tommy off. "I invited him Mama D."

"Really, then why are y'all back here whispering in the dark?" I realized Ms. Daniels always said someone was whispering in the dark when we were in plain view and the lights were on.

"Ms. D it is not dark out here and I was asking the same question."

"Well Thomas you need to be in there with your family not her." She turned and stormed off.

"What going on between you guys?"

"She's upset about us going on this trip without her."

"That's not it because Mr. Avery said they were moving to another state in a few weeks."

"When did he tell you he wanted to move out?"

"He's been talking about moving out for years but after Alonzo died he stopped but when you hired Ms. P he said after he sold Alonzo's house he was moving."

"I guess he didn't think about selling the house Naomi lived in until you guys got married." I whispered.

"That house sold faster than Alonzo's house."

"He turned down several buyers and took Alonzo's house of the market three times."

"Well he found a house yesterday so I guess he has to tell her soon and since we are moving you need..."

"Why are y'all still out here?" Ms. Daniels bellowed.

"We're on the way in." Tommy said. When we walked in Rodney walked over and sat next to me. "Is everything alright?"

"She's upset, so we'll talk about it later." Everyone talked and ate until about eight o'clock. "Okay kids it's time to get ready for bed." Ms. Daniels announced. Mr. Avery nodded so I wouldn't say anything. "Good night babies come give me a hug." They gave me a hug and I kissed them on the forehead.

Olivia grabbed some leftovers and ran out without saying bye or helping to clean up. "Well I'm not going to be like Olivia and just run off but I'm not going to clean up either so y'all have a good night." Tommy said winking at me as he, Naomi, and the kids went home. Mr. Avery announced,

"Well I have an early tee time so I'm going to bed. See you in the morning Alisha nice meeting you Rodney."

"Well Rodney I'll understand if you have to leave."

"No I'm going to help you clean up. He said smiling. "Thanks," I said as I picked up the empty boxes. We chatted about the center as we cleaned. I put the dishes in the dish washer Rodney took out the trash. He walked back in and looked around to see if we were done. "I guess that's it."

"It looks that way." I smiled.

"Well I guess I'll be going." He said gently caressing my cheek. "Rodney you can't do that." I said abruptly. "Do what I was wiping something off your cheek."

"Forgive me."

"You're forgiven." We laughed "So I guess I'll be heading out."

"Okay Rodney, be safe." I gave him a hug and as I released my embraced he pulled me closer and kissed me so I responded.

"Oh my goodness, please forgive me."

"No need to ask for forgiveness Alisha I knew what I was doing and I would like to do it again."

"Rodney you're engaged to Rebecca."

"Who told you I was engaged to her or was it the same person that told you was married?"

"Aren't you?"

"No we broke up months ago."

"Did you tell Tommy that?"

"Yes we talked about him going back home and Mr. Avery moving so my ugly breakup found its way into the conversation."

Rodney and I sat on the front porch and talked until about midnight.

□

...What's Next?

Six months after the planned moving day Tommy and Naomi were finally moving back to our home town permanently. His mom wasn't doing well so he had been going back and forth once he moved the family in until he completed his last project and trained his replacement for his job. Naomi looked as if she was due any day. Ms. Daniels moved in with Naomi to help out so Mr. Avery made the first move and rented my grandparents' house. Every house they found Ms. Daniels found an issue with it postponing Mr. Avery's plans. Ms. Daniels decided to move out of my house so they could be closer to Naomi. I did Naomi a favor and suggested they move into my grandparent's house because I knew she couldn't take her mother in the same house. My Uncle was doing better financially so he purchased his own home almost a year ago but kept my house up so it was renter ready.

About two weeks before Tommy was schedule to leave he was getting frustrated. When I pulled up Tommy was pacing back and forth on the porch. I rushed out of the car, "Tommy is everything alright?"

"No these folk won't let me retire."
"Man I thought something was wrong with Naomi."
"Well its stressing her out because Mama D keeps bugging her about what we are doing."
"Ms. Daniels has really surprised me."
"Now I see why Naomi wants her to move."
"Are you about to ask me to put them out?"
"Yes, but wait until we have the baby."
"Tommy that's another month or two away," I sighed.
"I know but you and Mr. Avery can come up with a plan because she's annoying."
"I know because she's not the woman I hired over ten years ago."
"I know and I accused Naomi of being too sensitive." Tommy grunted.
"Well, seeing is believing. I talked to Naomi last week and they're going on a cruise for five days."
"He has that kind of money?"
"No, I paid for it so he would have the

money for their new house."

"He told me yesterday he was thinking about moving into a retirement community because he's too old to take care of a house."

"I told him that two month ago when he was visiting his grandson."

"What was Ginger's baby's name anyway?"

"I forgot because they changed it and he doesn't really talk about him but goes up there twice a year to spend some time with the family."

"Well what happen when he was up there the last time."

"I don't know, why?"

"Naomi said when he came home he didn't talk to anybody for two days, he just sat in the study."

"I'm not sure but I think the wife is concerned about him giving information to Ginger because she sent a couple of letters."

"Why would she do that?"

"I think the husband is still dealing with her, so who would you blame?"

"I would never cheat on my wife so that's stupid to me."

"Me either but they do it."

"I guess you would know." We laughed as we walked into the house. "Tommy how long has he been here."

"Oh yea Rodney came over to see you after his trip."

"You suck."

"Well he was on the porch with me I guess he has jet lag."

"Where is Ms. Pye?"

"She said she was going to do some shopping before she goes on vacation. Alisha, who's going to take of the kids while she's gone," he asked looking nervous.

"I am."

"But you're still working."

"And I'm also my own boss."

"Never mind, my mind is just on my situation."

"Yeah right because it looks like you played golf this morning."

"Well the man hadn't played golf in over two months so I had to take him to play."

"Whatever Tommy. "

"You won't play with me."

"I'll play with you tomorrow."

"Are you serious?"

"If she going to play I'll be here for that tee time."

"Good afternoon Rodney." I smiled

"Hey baby girl." He said as he walked over to me and embraced my lips with the warm moisture of his passion filled lips. "I guess you really missed me huh."

"Yes I did and I was going to wait but I knew you were not working today so I came over here to surprise you."

"But Rodney I knew you would be here to take us to dinner."

"No Alisha I mean…" The kids ran in and cut our conversation short. "Mommy mommy, mommy," they screamed.

"Hello Millie, Julian, and Alonzo."

"Hello Mr. Rodney."

"Hi guys, how was school?"

"It was great they yelled."

"So where would you like to go for dinner?"

"Dogs Dogs," AJ yelled.

"No Hamburguesa Perfeccion!" JJ said. Millie looked at her brothers and shook her head. "We need to eat food not junk so I want to go to the new restaurant around the corner."

"Alisha that place is the truth." Tommy said eating a doughnut as he walked into the family room. "What kind of food do they have?" Rodney asked.

"It's southern on one side but Italian on the other side."

"So they sell both types."

"No, the Southern is a buffet but the Italian has a separate kitchen and dining area."

"Oh, so which one would you like?"

"I want Italian." Millie said.

"Well the men want southern." JJ shouted.

"Calm down let's get it to go and enjoy a nice meal here." Rodney suggested.

"That sounds like a great idea to me." I said. "I have the website pulled up so we can order." Tommy blurted.

"Who invited you Tommy?" I laughed. We ordered and paid so Tommy and the boys went to get the food. After the kids ate we watched a movie and they got ready for school. Rodney and I sat on the swing in the backyard and talked. Tommy disappeared during dinner so he could talk to Naomi.

Mr. Avery was getting tired of his bride being so clingy to everyone except him so he asked me to help him plan a honeymoon to rekindle the fire in their marriage. I paid for the vacation because I was concerned about their future and Ms. Daniels was wearing out her welcome with Naomi. Mr. Avery picked up Ms. Daniels that afternoon from Naomi's house. "Hi Alfred was the traffic bad coming over?"

"No I beat the school buses."

"What would you like for dinner tonight?"

"I'm taking you to and early dinner because I want to talk to you about something."

"Would it have anything to do with our anniversary next week," she giggled.

"Yes it does and you're going to love it."

"Well now I want to know."

"Are you sure?"

"Yes tell me Alfred."

"I booked us a five day cruise."

"A what?" She screamed. He sighed because he knew she was going to complain. "A cruise and we leave in two days"

"Alfred I'm so excited because we need this trip." He was shocked but she knew her presence at Naomi's home was unwanted. She figured her absence would cause Naomi to welcome her back. They ordered their food to go so they could plan and pack for the trip.

Tommy was listening to his wife complain about her mother. "Tommy she's driving me crazy."

"Have you asked her to give you some space."

"Tommy I can't do that didn't you see how she acted when Alisha took the kids on a family vacation without her."

"Yes but you are carrying my child so I refuse to allow you to be stressed out."

"I'm okay just a little frustrated."

"Have my parents been treating you right?"

"This is a great town I don't understand why you and Alisha left."

"We had our reasons."

"Your parents are awesome and the kids spend the weekend with them so they can go to church together."

"Do you go to church?"

"Yes Tommy I go with my Mama and Mr. Avery."

"Great so my parents like you?"

"Yes and I met your brother Marcus."

"What about my sisters?"

"I met them but they are a little different and they can't stand Alisha."

"I know they've been jealous of her since she was born but hated her because of me and Julian."

"Why?"

"She married him and told me to have a mind of my own."

"That's stupid so anyway when are you coming home?"

"I don't know because they gave me another project."

"But you gave them a thirty day notice"

"I know and the project was supposed to end tomorrow but the guy I'm working with isn't holding up his end of the bargain."

"Then let it lapse it will be on him."

"Baby you know I don't work like that I have to do everything in excellence as if I'm doing it for God."

"Baby I know you have to lead by example but you have a family that needs you."

"I want to be able to teach my children that they must give one hundred percent of themselves regardless of the job and my family isn't lacking anything."

"You're not here."

"I know but that was your idea so you have to live with your choice."

"Why are you being so mean Tommy?"

"Baby I'm not but I told you not to move until we sold the house but you were trying to get away from your mother instead of telling her the truth."

"That not fair, she was annoying you as well."

"But she's your mother not mine. If things were different it would've been settle a long time ago because I would never let anyone and I don't care who it is to disrespect my mate."

"Tommy I'm getting off the phone because you are upset and it's causing you to lash out at me."

"This has to do with the fact that you can't handle truth."

"Good-bye Thomas."

"Baby, don't be upset let's work this out."

"No Thomas." She hung up the phone and

when he called back she sent him to voicemail.

Tommy walk out the door, "Alisha we need to talk."

"What's up?"

"It's Naomi she's upset because I told her the truth."

"Tommy I keep telling you it's almost impossible for a woman to accept the truth."

"Yea we know." The men laughed.

Rodney asked, "Alisha why are women always asking for this or that kind of man but they don't bring the same values or qualities they want a man to have."

"Yeah I can screw anything but I want a quality woman to carry my last name."

"Well we have flaws." I stated.

"I don't care about the mistakes she's made in the past I just want her to complement me when we're together" Rodney said as he winked at me.

"I know man, and these down low church hoes I keep meeting are getting on my nerves; sorry Alisha I mean church whores."

"Sitting up in church like they're so perfect and screwing out of both draw legs."

"Dang Tommy I haven't heard that one in a long time but you're right."

"Okay boys you can stop venting now." I said.

"No Alisha because as a Pastor I'm tired of women throwing themselves at me. I'm the one that should be finding a wife."

"If they spent as much time working on themselves to become a wife instead of creating traps preying on men they might find something worth having."

"Or stop giving it up so easy thinking it's a secret but God can see everything they do."

"You know they think if the other church folk don't see it or they dress it up like a prayer God can't see their indiscretions."

"You mean sin. Call it what it is."

"You guys are funny." I laughed and found an exit.

"Alisha, Rodney caught old girl in her office

at the church with the deacon's wife."
Tommy shouted.

"Wait whose old girl?" I quickly turned back around.

"Thomas I didn't tell her the cause of the break-up."

"Our tee time is at eight thirty."

"Oh so now you want to change the subject."

"Can I talk to her alone so I can explain the situation Thomas?"

"I'll get a couple of beers while you talk, Alisha do you want any...never mind."

"Tommy doesn't have to leave but you can get me a peach tea."

"Yes ma'am." Tommy said as he apologized to Rodney. "Tommy it's okay because I'm not upset and I know what you're doing." I laughed.

While Tommy was in the house Rodney grabbed my hand. "Baby, Rebecca cheated on me with the head Deacons wife but they felt as if it wasn't cheating because it was oral."

"Wait your future first lady was having an affair at the church with the head Deacon's wife."

"Well they had just gotten married so they were newlyweds."

"That's crazy but I guess we make excuses to satisfy our flesh even if it goes against what we believe and no one can see it."

"Alisha it was painful and I tried to work it out but what would she do if I was on a mission trip."

"I know so did you tell Jamaal?"

"No I told her to do it."

"Did she?"

"Yes but he was cool with it."

"I forgot the male fantasy."

"It was that, the fact that that the women had been abstaining for a while, and they had not slept with men."

"So when did it happen?"

"Two days before that kiss that caused me to do this..." Rodney reached for my hand.

"Really so she was a rebound?" Tommy said as he walked out the door with our drinks.

"No, Alisha was not my rebound."

"Thanks Rodney but I think he knows that." We continued to talk until Rodney looked at his watch. Tommy and I talked until the wee hours of the night on my terrace.

I opened my eyes just before dawn and Tommy was lying on my lap. I eased him off and went downstairs to cook breakfast. At seven I woke the kids up so they could get ready for school. "Good morning mommy," Millie moaned. "I'll get the boys up so you can finish breakfast."

"Thanks baby." I said kissing Millie on the forehead. When I finished cooking Ms. Pye came in. "Good morning Alisha."

"Good morning Ms. Pye." The kids were at the table within fifteen minutes. The boys gave me a hug as they greeted us. "Good morning Alisha," Tommy said when he came downstairs. "Alisha did you make any coffee?"

"No but Ms. Pye is making it now."

"Good because I slept hard."

"Well you went to sleep outside on my lounge chair."

"I think it was the four beers I had."

"Tommy you drank four beers!"

"I know but I was upset about Naomi."

"Rodney will be here in a few minutes so are you going to play with us?"

"Yes. Everyone put your dishes in the dishwasher oh and Tommy will you get my clubs out of the storage closet in the garage." Rodney got there at eight o'clock and we left out fifteen minutes later. We played the back nine because Tommy had a meeting. After we got our feelings hurt by Tommy, Rodney and I went to eat at Undercover Dishes.

After our late lunch we went to my office. I had to unlock the door because Olivia was not in which was strange. "Come on in and make yourself at home."
"I'm going in your office to take a nap."
"That's cool I have some work to do anyway." Rodney went to sleep. I checked my email before checking and confirming my appointments and meetings for the following week. I linked the new information to my cell phone calendar. I sat there replying to emails and making calls. At three Olivia walked in and handed me some mail. "Doc how long have you been here?"
"For a little over an hour and keep your voice down because Rodney's in the back asleep."
"Oh I had to take some documents to the Community Center."

"I was wondering where you were."
"Do you need anything?"
"No but didn't you take that paperwork over there last week?"
"Yes but Mrs. Margret was the only one that didn't sign the paperwork because she was out sick so she called me this morning and

I took her the paperwork." I put it in the file with the other paperwork." Olivia walked out. I knew she was hiding something but my vow to stay out other people's stuff cause me to keep my mouth closed, so I allowed that thought to fade away. "I must say your sofa is comfortable."

"I know but the bed is even better." I laughed.

"It's a bed back there?"

"Yes on your right."

"I was so sleepy that I lay down on the first soft thing I saw."

"I saw so are you ready to leave?"

"I'm ready whenever you are."

"Well I have to get home and get dinner ready."

"Okay just let me know and I found this under the sofa." It was the envelop Dawn gave me from Donna but I never read it. I looked at the letter fearful of what it would tell me and decided to read it later. "I'll read it later because I need to get home and prepare dinner."

"Can I join you for dinner?"

"That is a question you should ask the kids."

"Alright, we need to make a stop so I can have leverage."

"What are you going to do?"

"It's a secret so I think I'll drop you off first."

"You're not right."

"No this is wisdom." We laughed as we drove off. Rodney dropped me off and after opening my door and walking me into the house he ran off. Ten minutes later the kids ran in screaming their greeting. I gave them a hug and told them to put their things up.

"Hi Ms. Pye how are you this evening?"

"I'm great but you seem to be on cloud nine."

"My life is finally calm."

"So Rodney is the one?"

"It has nothing to do with my outside relationships but my spiritual relationship is just right so everything around me has fallen into place."

"Well the kids seem to love Rodney so if he is the one they're on board."

"Thanks Ms. Pye and here's your weekly reward."

"Wait this isn't right."

"I threw something in because I heard you went shopping and I know you're going on vacation."

"Alisha this is too much."

"Ms. Pye you've been a rock and constant help to this family and my friends so thank you."

"Well I'm not going to block my blessings, thank you baby."

"Thank you Ms. Pye." She walked out the door smiling. Rodney came in ten minutes later with grocery bags. The kids were doing homework in the family room. He walked in saying, "Hello guys."

"Hi Mr. Rodney." they said in unison

"I wanted to know if I could stay for dinner?"

"Mr. Rodney, are you sweet on our Mama." Millie asked looking up at him. He was speechless but gave her an answer anyway.

"Yes as a matter of fact I would like to ask her..."

"Okay it's time to wash up for dinner." I announced. "Mommy you interrupted him but you can stay for dinner." The boys had already run into the bathroom to wash up.

"Forgive me Rodney but I didn't know you were back."

"I just walked in and realized I didn't have to bribe them they said I can stay."

"What did you buy them?"

"I bought fixings to make Sundaes after dinner."

"Fixings really, I guess you've been around Tommy and Mr. Avery too long."

"Don't forget I'm a country boy." We laughed. After dinner the kids got ready for bed as we cleaned up the kitchen. Rodney and I were sitting on the porch when he got a call causing him to leave suddenly.

While on their cruise Ms. Daniel agreed to move into a Senior Community as long as they didn't move into a high-rise. "Are you sure about this Sarah because I don't want you to change your mind once you see the baby."
"I won't Alfred because the past two days have been like a dream and I'm ready to live my life for me."
"That's great and I think we need to go back to our room and celebrate that revelation."
"There's only one stipulation to the agreement."
"What's that?"
"Alisha keeps sending us on these awesome vacations for our anniversary."
"I'm sure she will." They laughed as they retired to their room for the entire day enjoying the love they shared for one another. They decided to extend their vacation so they traveled for two weeks before going on a second two week cruise. Their flight home was peaceful and their passion had been rekindled so they were a little adventurous on the plane. After they landed Ms. Daniels called the house for someone to pick them up. Tommy was

texting Mr. Avery to let them know Naomi was in labor. "Sarah we have to get a rental car."

"Why Albert is Thomas busy?"

"Naomi is in labor." She started screaming. "Sarah we can call Alisha when we get to the rental place."

"Albert you know Thomas called her first." She said breathing heavily as they quickly rushed to the car rental booth. When they got to the hospital Tommy's parents and the kids were there waiting. "Where is she," Ms. Daniels asked frantically. "They just took her to a room where she's being prepped and they'll let us know when we can see her." The nurse came out and let them know only four people could be in the room at a time. Ms. Daniels, Jasmine, and Lois decided to join Tommy in the delivery room. Jasmine texted her brother the events as they happened in the room keeping the waiting room crowd and me up to date. Two hours later everyone was ready to meet the seven pound eighteen inch Camille Rose. She was a welcomed addition to their new family.

We flew home that weekend to meet Tommy's newest addition. We got there around nine Friday night rented a car and got two rooms at the best hotel in town.

"Babe I'm going to call Tommy and let him know we are here."

"Call Mama D first," Millie begged as the boys chimed in. "Rodney will you call Tommy while I call Ms. Daniels."

"Yes baby." We made our calls as we drove off. We never made it to our rooms because I wanted to see the baby and the kids wanted to see their grandparents. "Hi Ms. Daniels we just got into town and the kids want to see you."

"Albert the kids are here." She yelled.

"Bring them to our house they can stay with us."

"Okay we will be there in about fifteen minutes."

"Okay." She was so excited that she hung up without saying good bye. "Baby we are going to drop the kids off first." I said to Rodney.

"Okay but it's going to be late when we pick them up."

"Don't worry about that and take a left at the light."

We were at the house in no time. Mr. Avery was on the porch waiting for us. The kids jumped out of the car screaming, "Mama D, Pops." I Got out of the car and hugged Mr. Avery as he helped Rodney get the kids suitcases. I walked up on the porch and hugged Ms. Daniels, "I'm going over to Tommy's to see the baby before it gets too late."

"She's a beautiful bundle of joy."

"Congratulations Mama D," I said as I hugged her before I ran back to the car. When we pulled up to Tommy's house it was quiet so I called him to let him know we were outside. Tommy came out as we were walking up the steps. "Tommy, how are you?"

"I'm good. Hey Rodney I didn't know you were coming." Rodney widened his eyes to signal Tommy so he would stop talking.

"Come on in the baby is in the living room." I walked into the room and looked at the baby, "Tommy she's beautiful."

"Man you're blessed." Rodney said as he shook his hand and patted him on the back. "I just wanted to see Naomi but since she's not feeling well I'll come over tomorrow."

"Where are the kids?"

"Ms. Daniels has them."

"So you are going to be alone in a hotel?"

"We have separate rooms."

"Don't slip because this is the perfect set up."

"Man I know and if I hadn't paid for the room I would stay somewhere else." Rodney said shaking his head while looking at me.

"Come on baby we won't slip."

"I pray we don't."

"You don't have self-control?"

"Alisha you know it's not always that simple at certain times." Tommy whispered.

"I know I was just kidding." I said kissing Rodney on the cheek. He pushed me off.

"I'll be back in the morning."

"Okay Alisha." We walked towards the car and I started feeling little different. As we drove off I cut on the radio and it was the right music for the perfect set up. Rodney reached over and gently caressed my hand. I leaned back in my seat and closed my eyes. I enjoyed my alone time with him.

"Baby we're here."

"I guess I fell asleep," I said stretching.

"Come let's get some rest because I know you're going to have me running all over town tomorrow." Rodney got the bags out of the car and opened my door. We went to the second floor. He opened my door and as he carried the bags in he check the room out before I went in. "Everything seems to be alright."

"Thanks baby," I said as I walked into the room. I kissed him lovingly on his inviting lips to show my appreciation. Rodney grabbed me as he skillfully parted my lips with the warmth of his tongue. Rodney and I were in the bed within seconds and pulling off our clothes when my phone rung but I ignored it. Within minutes Rodney's phone started ringing as he parted my legs drawing his attention. "Alisha, I have to get out of here. He pulled up his pants and put my key on the desk. "Baby I'm sorry." he said as he rushed out the door. I called Tommy back, "Thanks Tommy."

"I saw the look he had in his eyes and I know you so I'm just trying to keep you honest before you get married."

"Tommy how did you and Naomi keep from slipping?"

"We," He paused. "Alisha this is Rodney let me call you back." He hung up before answering the question or I could respond. We went over the next morning and spent time with them. We had lunch with everyone including Tommy's family. We caught a four o'clock flight back home because Rodney had to preach on Sunday.

Naomi and Tommy decided that he would work part time for the company but only as an independent contractor. He became the Elder over the four churches so his father could groom him to be the Bishop. Tommy made a promise to Naomi to give his family one full day, five weeks of vacation a year, and a date night every two weeks. Naomi became a house wife and Tommy agreed to the stipulations required by his wife in order to take the jobs he had. Tommy decided to stay at my house when he came to town on business so he could bring the family. A few months later Ms. Daniels and Mr. Avery moved into their new home which was an hour and a half away from Naomi.

I was not welcomed at Rodney's Church because the women thought I was the reason for the break-up of him and Rebecca. We got ready Sunday morning but the children seemed unhappy. AJ pouted as we ate breakfast. "Okay you guys seem so unhappy what's wrong?"
"Everybody is gone." Julian said as he played with his food. "Mommy we miss our friends and Papa Avery." AJ said with his head on the table.
"Mommy we didn't realize how much we missed everybody until we saw them and you need a husband."
"Wait, how did we go from missing everybody to me needing a husband?"

"Well we are going to grow up so you need a companion to keep you company."
"You've been around your grandparents to long Millie"

"Mommy, Mr. Rodney likes you so you should marry him."

"They're right Alisha you should."

"Rodney?" I turned around to him on one knee with an open box. I looked at the kids with tear stained eyes as they cheered and I stood up. Rodney walked over to me and slid the ring onto my shaking finger. "You will forever be my first lady." The kids ran over and hugged us. Did we do it right Mr. Rodney?" AJ asked.

"So y'all set me up?"

"Yes we did."

"But when did you do it?"

"After the night we had sundaes with Ms. Pye and Uncle T's help." Millie said. I thought about his congregation and shivered. "Is everything alright?"

"Yes Babe," I kissed Rodney on the cheek remembering God's love for us to grow and allowing us to be uncomfortable is the first step. Our faith in Him is strengthened through trials and tribulation so as I go through He is with me or waiting for me on the other side.

When we got to church the nasty looks and eye rolling started because Rodney walked in with me and sat me in the front row before he went into his office. He had already escorted the children to the youth

department. He sat next to me during the
service. This day had been planned for
weeks but I didn't know it. After the service
was over he asked everyone to stay seated.
"I've been planning this day for a while and
as my congregation I want you to meet my
first lady." He held his hand out towards
me. "I asked this woman that I've known for
over twenty years to marry me this morning
and she said yes." He smiled and kissed me
on the cheek. Thomas Ponder and Mr.
Avery will you come forth," I started crying
because I knew what was about to happen.
The kids walked in and sat on the front
pew. "Today is my last day being a single
man." Rebecca walked out and the deacon's
wife stood to follow her but quickly sat
down after seeing her husband's face.
Tommy took the microphone and within ten
minutes we were Mr. and Dr. Rodney
Mitchell. Rodney had preached a sermon on
Pure Love. After service the congregation
had cake, punch, and finger foods so we
could have a meet and greet before left the
Church. We had dinner with Tommy and
Mr. Avery at Jake's, so Jerri as usual
invited himself, before it was time for their
flight.

Mr. Avery worked out his issues with his
grandson's mother. The Avery's time was

spent traveling, visiting their grandchildren at least four times a year, and letting them stay a few weeks during the summer. Tommy's parents were overjoyed because he was the only child that had children close to them. Until Marcus moved back and took over the funeral home there but kept his business in Louisiana. The sister's never got married but chased men and had affairs. My Uncle Junior wanted to retire so that brought on a family meeting about the garage and towing company.

Rodney and I decided to sell the house Julian bought because we wanted to create our own memories so we thought about moving into his house. I worked at the Community Center part time and over saw the churches counseling center. As I was going through some papers I found that unread letter, so I put it in my purse. When I got home I pulled the letter out to read it but the kids distracted me so I jumped up and knocked over my bag the letter fell out of the bag. I forgot about the letter again. We at dinner and the kids prepared for bed. Rodney and I sat on the terrace looking at the stars and reminiscing. "Baby I'm getting sleepy." I said stretching. "You go on in I'll meet you in a minute I have to look at something.

While we were in bed Rodney asked, "What have you been doing today?"

"Cleaning out my office so I can put some files in storage."

"Did you come across some things you needed to settle?"

"Not that I know of," I said thinking.

"So what's this?" He handed me the letter I had yet to read again. This forced me to read it. As I read the letter my worst fears were now a revelation. Rodney caressed my face as he raised my head. "Baby what's wrong?"

"Rodney he's..." He placed his hand over my mouth. "I know baby we're going to get through this together."

In 2012 after a life changing circumstances and overwhelming revelation she was reminded that she was a precious gem protected by God. This revelation birthed Alisha Coleman the Author and Poet. In December of 2012 after completing her first book, If Your Wife Is So Good...Why Are You In The Bed With Me?(Holloman, 2013), she knew that was the beginning of her ability to tell stories about overcoming life's obstacles. While the first book was being edited the urge to write a second book was brewing causing the series The Clean-Up Woman Chronicles to be born. Being a Poet there was a need to not only write but to speak on the issues within the book; which included abuse, rape, and cheating so others could grasp the pain and hurt endured by so many silent voices. The need birthed 'Alisha Speaks' a poetic soundtrack for the signature book "If Your Wife Is So Good...".

Alisha means several things but in 2012 I was protected by God. Coleman is an occupational name that was given to men that gathered charcoal (coal). It has been said that coal under an unnatural heat and pressure produces a diamond; which is why Alisha Coleman is a pressure gem. The surname can also mean "dove" in Latin. This is why Alisha Coleman is trying to take flight to find peace.

If Your Wife Is So Good...

Follows a woman refusing to accept or acknowledge the pain she's carried from childhood. She seeks out unavailable men for brief flings to protect her heart. The only issue is that the men are good so her flings linger. Alisha finally meets the man of her dreams. She falls in love which causes confusion in her strangely comfortable lifestyle. Alisha chronicles her exploits with an array of unavailable men, as she searches for the one who will make her heart leap. Throughout her journey Alisha struggles with her physical desires for men versus her faith and morals.

Really was created to assist women on examining their actions and reactions, while reflecting on their heart condition. We all struggle with facing the truth about ourselves and taking constructive criticism is a struggle but growing takes pruning. So prune yourself with this short self-reflection question and answer booklet.

- Have you been broken

- Do you fear success

- Do you love yourself

- Have you settled for the wrong mate

www.ingramcontent.com/pod-product-compliance
Lightning Source LLC
Chambersburg PA
CBHW022159260626
47155CB00019B/3360